I0579756

GRYPHON PRECINCT

Also by Keith R.A. DeCandido,
from eSpec Books

The Precinct Series
DRAGON PRECINCT
UNICORN PRECINCT
GOBLIN PRECINCT
TALES FROM DRAGON PRECINCT

Coming Soon
MERMAID PRECINCT

Forthcoming Titles
PHOENIX PRECINCT
MANTICORE PRECINCT
MORE TALES FROM DRAGON PRECINCT

Other Titles
WITHOUT A LICENSE

GRYPHON PRECINCT

Keith R.A. DeCandido

eBooks

Pennsville, NJ

PUBLISHED BY
eSpec Books LLC
Danielle McPhail, Publisher
PO Box 242,
Pennsville, New Jersey 08070
www.especbooks.com

Copyright 2013, 2018 Keith R.A. DeCandido

ISBN: 978-1-942990-88-8
ISBN (ebook): 978-1-942990-87-1

All rights reserved. No part of the contents of this book may
be reproduced or transmitted in any form or by any means without
the written permission of the publisher.

All persons, places, and events in this book are fictitious
and any resemblance to actual persons, places, or events is purely
coincidental.

Interior Design: Danielle McPhail
Sidhe na Daire Multimedia
www.sidhenadaire.com

Cover Art and Gryphon Medallion: Mike McPhail
www.mcp-concepts.com

Art Credits - www.Fotolia.com
Sword © michelaubryphoto

*Dedicated to the memory of
Dorina DiLullo, a bright light dimmed
too soon. Rest in peace, my dear friend.*

ACKNOWLEDGMENTS

For the new edition:
Many thanks to Danielle Ackley-McPhail, Mike McPhail, and Greg Schauer of eSpec Books, and additional thanks to Meredith Peruzzi for general wonderfulness.

Also thanks to the character of Aleta lothLathna, originally intended as a one-off for the "Catch and Release" story in *Tales from Dragon Precinct*, but who, in the writing of this book forced herself into a much larger role.

From the original edition:

As ever, I must give thanks and praise to Neal Levin of Dark Quest Books, who has kept the flame of this series burning, to Elektra Hammond, my ever-reliable editor, and Lucienne Diver, my magnificent agent.

Gratitude also to the usual suspects: Wrenn Simms, GraceAnne Andreassi DeCandido, Tina Randleman, Dale Mazur, Laura Anne Gilman, *Shihan* Paul and the rest of the folks at the dojo, and my fellow members of the Liars Club.

Also to the furry ones, especially Rhiannon, who died of mouth cancer while I was writing this book, and Kaylee, the new, adorable black kitten.

PROLOGUE

This distressed his chamberlain, Sir Rommett, no end, because Lord Albin was never late for the first appointment of the day.

Oh, as the day wore on, the lord of the demesne's ability to be punctual deteriorated, and engagements scheduled for the end of the day were postponed about a third of the time. As the person who ruled the city-state of Cliff's End, Lord Albin was in great demand. (Technically, he co-ruled with his wife, Lady Meerka, but she limited herself to overseeing financial matters. Her husband had to deal with everything else.)

That Lord Albin had agreed to see Sir Rommett first thing in the morning underlined the importance of the meeting. To make matters worse, Rommett had no idea what the meeting was about. Lord Albin had been unusually mysterious, saying only that it was "a grave matter."

When the time chimes rang nine times, Rommett decided to take action. Normally, one waited for the lord to arrive at his leisure. To do aught else would be highly improper, and Rommett prided himself on his propriety. But Lord Albin was now an hour late, and worse, had sent no notice of his tardiness.

Stepping out of his office, he saw his secretary sitting at his desk, writing on a scroll. "Bertram, has there been any word from Lord Albin?"

Looking up from his writing, Bertram said, "I'm afraid not, sir."

"He's an hour late."

"Yes sir, he is."

"No message, nothing?"

Bertram shook his head. "No, sir."

"Damn. This is very unlike him, don't you think, Bertram?"

"I would never presume to say, sir. His scribe did come by."

"What, that gnome?" Rommett asked with a frown.

Nodding, Bertram said, "Yes, sir. He hadn't seen his lordship yet this morning, despite having gone by his office twice. I sent a pageboy to check with the house faerie, and his lordship did get up and leave his bedroom at seven this morning, along with Lady Meerka. They had breakfast together, and then her ladyship went to the eastern wing to speak with the magickal examiner. I'm not sure where his lordship went, I'm sorry to say."

"Odd business. The meeting with the guild leaders is still at half past nine, yes?"

"Yes, sir."

"We'll never be able to reschedule that." Rommett shuddered. Finding a time when the leaders of all the guilds that controlled various occupations throughout Cliff's End could meet had been almost impossible. Postponing and finding a new time would take weeks, and the guilds had already been threatening work stoppages if they didn't get to meet with Rommett soon. "If he's not in his bedchambers and he's not in his office, he's likely in the sitting room."

"Yes, sir."

"I'm going to have to check there myself. If he *is* there, it's best he not be disturbed by a mere pageboy."

Bertram's eyes widened with shock. "Is that—is that *wise*, sir?"

"We'll find out soon enough, won't we?" Rommett sighed. "It's just so unlike him not to send word if he's *this* late."

"Yes, sir." Bertram sounded dubious, but Rommett studiously ignored him and started down the corridor toward Lord Albin's sitting room. He noticed that the guard who was usually posted near Rommett's office wasn't present. Indignant, Rommett whirled around to face his secretary again. "Bertram! Where is the guard?"

"I'm afraid the guards assigned to the castle are a bit short-handed this morning, sir. Today is the funeral."

Bertram had said that as if Rommett would know what funeral he was referring to.

Apparently deciphering the quizzical expression Rommett gave him, Bertram continued: "One of the lieutenants in the Castle Guard was killed during that, ah, unfortunate incident at the bank."

Rommett vaguely remembered a report about something like that. In fact, thinking about it, he recalled a requisition from Captain Osric for permission to promote one of the guards to lieutenant to replace the detective in question—Hawk, was it? He still hadn't approved that requisition. In any case, while the chamberlain was not happy at the notion of the castle being short-handed of protection, he also was not so churlish as to deny people the right to attend the funeral of a comrade. "I assume this funeral will not extend past lunch?"

"No, sir," Bertram said confidently.

"Very well." Nodding, Rommett again turned his back on his secretary and proceeded through the castle halls until he reached Lord Albin's study.

The double doors at the end of the corridor were closed. That was meaningless in and of itself, as the doors were rarely open. If Lord Albin was inside, it was usually a meeting that he did not wish people to eavesdrop on (more public meetings were held in the dining room or in his office); if he wasn't inside the doors were not just closed, but locked.

Rommett hesitated, then knocked.

There was no response.

Praying to Temisa that he was not making a career-ending mistake, he grabbed the left-hand door and pulled down the handle. The door creaked as Rommett gingerly pulled it open to reveal Lord Albin sitting in the plush chair, currently turned to face the fireplace, which was roaring, as it was a chill autumn day. Lord Albin hadn't been well lately, and in retrospect, Rommett shouldn't have been surprised that his lordship had decided to take refuge in front of a fire.

Oddly, Lord Albin was simply staring straight ahead, as if lost in thought. He had an odd expression on his face, but Rommett couldn't figure out for the life of him what precisely was odd about it, merely that it was.

"My lord, I'm sorry, but we were supposed to meet an hour ago to discuss that—that grave matter of yours, and I need to meet with the guild leaders in just half an hour, so I was hoping . . ."

Rommett trailed off, as Lord Albin had made no response of any kind to his chamberlain's words. In fact, he hadn't blinked, hadn't moved, hadn't twitched his mouth, hadn't done *anything*.

Not even breathe.

His voice a strangled whisper, Rommett said, "Oh, Temisa, no . . ."

Hesitantly, he approached the body. Afraid to touch it, he instead just looked at it. Lord Albin's eyes stared unblinkingly ahead, his body as still as a statue. Rommett briefly felt dizzy and had to steady himself on the frame of the fireplace—only to quickly remove his hand and almost fall forward, as the bricks were hot from the fire.

Filled with a sudden urge to be away from the sitting room as fast as possible, Rommett turned and practically ran, his legs carrying him toward the main entrance to the castle. Only as he entered the vestibule did he realize that his legs knew where to take him even when his conscious mind did not: Bertram had said that Lady Meerka was with Boneen, the magickal examiner, and his lair was in the basement of the eastern wing of the castle.

Coming in through the main entrance at the same time were two members of the Castle Guard, a human man and a half-human, half-elven woman. They wore black leather armor as all guards did. A medallion on the chest included a stylized gryphon, the family crest of Lord Albin and Lady Meerka, indicating that they were assigned to the castle. They both wore earth-colored cloaks with the same crest, the color denoting them as lieutenants in the Guard. Rommett could not remember their names.

The male half of the pair had a thick red beard and long red hair, which obscured all but his aquiline nose and penetrating eyes. He looked concerned upon seeing Rommett, and the chamberlain realized that his devastation was etched on his features.

"Sir Rommett," he asked, "are you all right?"

Flexing his hand, which still burned from the fireplace frame, Rommett said, "No. None of us may ever be all right again."

"What's wrong?"

Rommett hesitated, as if saying it made it more real.

Then he looked down at his hand, which was starting to get red. Saying it or not saying it would have no effect on anything, he forced himself to admit. Temisa had already taken him away.

"Lord Albin," he finally said, "is dead."

Both detectives' eyes went wide, and the half-elven detective, who was one of the ugliest women Rommett had ever seen—not just in face, but also in personality, as the woman had *no* respect for her betters—put her hand to the hilt of her sword, hanging from a belt scabbard. "How was he killed?"

Rommett stared at the woman for a second — Tresyllione, that was her name. "He wasn't *killed*! He's been ill, and he died in his sitting room."

"You're sure?" Tresyllione asked insistently. "His body had no markings on it, no indication of foul play?"

"Of course not, don't be ridiculous!" Rommett shook his head, wondering why he had even stopped to talk to these two idiots. "I must go inform Lady Meerka."

Flexing his left hand some more, he made a mental note to see a healer after he talked to her ladyship.

He also wondered if he wasn't too snappish with Tresyllione and her partner. In fact, he didn't investigate the body all *that* closely, and it was Lord Albin himself who proclaimed the law that any time someone died in Cliff's End, it should be investigated by the Castle Guard.

But no. His lordship had been sick. That was all.

ONE

LIEUTENANT TORIN BAN WYVALD STOOD AT ATTENTION OUTSIDE WHAT USED to be Lord Albin's office in the castle. He and the other highest-ranking members of the Castle Guard stood along one wall of the corridor outside the massive wooden door with a gryphon crest carved into it. That crest matched the one on Torin's armor and his cloak. They were lined up in order of rank, and within rank by seniority, so Captain Osric stood closest to the door, followed by Lieutenant Iaian, then Torin's partner Danthres Tresyllione, then Torin himself, with Lieutenants Dru and Grovis on Torin's left.

Osric had actually shaved, marking the first time Torin could recall having an unimpeded view of the captain's cheeks and chin since he was cut during the battle at Faf's Ridge and the healer cut off the stubble. Torin was amused to see that Osric kept rubbing his chin with obvious annoyance.

Across from them on the facing wall were ten men and two women dressed in gray armor and bright green capes. They were the highest-ranking members of the Royal Guard, who had accompanied King Marcus and Queen Marta. The rulers of the human lands had travelled from Velessa to Cliff's End to attend Lord Albin's funeral. It was a credit to how much the king and queen respected the late lord that they dropped everything and travelled immediately here, arriving in a week's time, the fastest a large group could traverse the distance between city-states on horseback. At the moment, the monarchs were behind the big wooden door with Lady Meerka.

"How much longer you think it's gonna be?" Dru muttered to Torin.

Torin smiled. "They are hardly likely to start the funeral without them, so they may take as long as they wish."

"Yeah, I know, it's just—" Dru sighed. "I wanna get this over with. Too many damn funerals."

Torin nodded. He and Danthres had just returned from the service for Dru's partner when Lord Albin's death was announced a week ago.

"Although I gotta admit, I'm lookin' forward to seein' Jayka Park."

From the other side of Torin, Danthres said, "It's just a clearing in the forest that's covered in grass."

"Nonsense," Grovis said from the other side of Dru, "it's quite lovely, and very expansive. It's also the only space large enough for such an event as this."

"Okay, I get why *he's* been in the park, bein' all upper-class an' shit." Dru jerked a thumb at Grovis, who was a scion of the family that owned the Cliff's End Bank. "But when were you ever in Jayka, Danthres?"

"It was the last time the king and queen were in the city-state— about eleven years ago. They were on their way to that festival on Saptor Isle for the prince, and they stayed here for two days, and we had to guard those ridiculous games they held in the monarchs' honor."

Osric chuckled. "That used to be the sort of thing the Castle Guard did all the time, especially before Albin took over. Lieutenants would spend the vast majority of their time standing in hallways like this waiting for the nobility to go somewhere and be escorted."

"A much more literal Castle Guard?" Torin grinned.

"Well, that was kinda the original point," Dru said. "I mean, Cliff's End used to be just this castle, back in Lord Jethro's day. The Castle Guard was just supposed to guard the castle. Hell, that's why Jayka Park's there."

Torin had thought his knowledge of the history of Cliff's End to be complete, but this was a surprise to him. "How so?"

"Well, back in the old days, everyone lived in the castle, so when they decided to go huntin' or ridin' or whatever, they'd just go out into the area between the castle and the port. But then people started buildin' houses and stuff, and people were puttin' their mansions in what used to be the huntin' and ridin' area—where Unicorn is now. So Jethro's son, Lord Jayka, he cleared out a piece'a the Forest of Nimvale to be the new park—and named it after himself, o'course."

"Yeah," Iaian said, "but it's only for the rich and stupid."

"Except on special occasions like this," Osric added. "Grovis is right, half the population of Cliff's End will be at this funeral. It's the only way to accommodate them."

"And it's a security nightmare," Danthres muttered. "Especially since the Brotherhood refused to rent us the magick detectors."

"They didn't need to," came a voice from across the hall. Looking over, Torin saw a smile on the person standing directly across from Osric. He was a tall, wiry human with a thick blond mustache. Where the others all had a symbol of a tree leaf over their hearts, the leader had a symbol of a short-sword in that place. Torin recalled Osric wearing a similar symbol on his armor during the war. This man was a general in the Royal Guard, while the remaining eleven were captains. "We brought our own. The king and queen go nowhere without magickal protection. Any unauthorized weapons or magick will be found out. Everything will be fine."

"I hope so." Danthres spoke in a sour tone that Torin knew all too well.

"Truly, Lieutenant," the general said confidently, "there is no cause for concern. In addition to the detectors, there is a full garrison of the Royal Guard here as well as a rather impressive number of your Castle Guard. Nothing untoward could possibly happen."

Osric scowled, and rubbed his bare chin. "I fought in the elven war, General, and I've been running the Castle Guard for over a decade, and those two experiences have shown me that there isn't anything that can't possibly happen."

"The crowd out there's nuts, too," Dru added. "We've been gettin' people pourin' into the damn city-state. Everyone wants t'pay their respects."

The general gave what Torin felt was an unnecessarily snide smile. "I expect that criminal activity has increased with all the added population?"

Taking pleasure in getting rid of that smile, Torin replied: "Actually, such activity has decreased. Lord Albin was very well respected, even by the criminal element of Cliff's End." He didn't add that half the population was recovering from their addiction to a designer drug, nor that the Guard had been particularly aggressive with the unlawful element since Hawk died.

Dru shook his head. "Yeah, mostly it's just screwing with commerce. Half the businesses are more active, the other half have practically shut down."

Torin winced. He knew that Dru's wife Zan's child-care business was suffering, as several of the children she usually cared for were being pressed into work for those businesses that were more active, and several others didn't require Zan's services because they had shut down and so could keep their kids at home. Already angered by the death of his partner, Zan's troubles had made Dru challenge Danthres for most pissed-off person in the squadroom.

The door with the gryphon crest suddenly opened, and three people exited the office. The first two, walking side by side, were a short, stout man and a tall, ethereal woman. They were in fact the same height, but it always appeared to Torin that the broad-shouldered King Marcus was shorter than his wife. Queen Marta also had much better posture than her husband, which aided in the illusion. Torin had, of course, been in the same room as the king and queen many times during the war, though he'd never gotten this close nor been introduced.

Torin noted that the king's beard — which was thick and brown during the war — was now trimmed to a small goatee, with his hair also cut much closer to his scalp than it had been a decade ago. The greatly reduced hair was no doubt due in part to how much gray was now in it. The king also had a misshapen nose, the result of being broken during the battle at Hobgoblin's Run, and large ears. A glamour would have concealed both the nose and the gray hair, but the king apparently chose not to use one.

The same could not be said for his queen. Marta's face was magnificently beautiful, with deep brown eyes, full red lips, and exquisitely coiffed hair that were all far too perfect to be anything but the product of magick.

One step behind them was the even shorter and stouter Lady Meerka. Like the other two, she wore all black, the color of mourning. Torin noted that, though Lord Albin had always, as far as he knew, worshipped Wiate, his widow did not wear a black rose in her hair, as was traditional for women of that faith grieving for their dead husbands.

As soon as the door had opened, all the guards, both royal and castle, stood at attention.

"You're sure you won't reconsider, Lady Meerka?" the king was saying as they came across the threshold.

"Quite sure, Your Highness." Meerka was almost shuddering as she spoke. "I have no interest in the inanity of politics. Numbers, at least, I can make sense of. People remain a mystery, and I fear I will drive the city-state to ruin if left to run it. My son can handle things just fine."

Torin frowned. He had assumed that Lady Meerka would take over the full governing of Cliff's End. She had been handling the city-state's finances ever since the crash a little under a decade ago, and indeed was at least partly responsible for the economic prosperity that the demesne had enjoyed since. But all he knew about Blayk, their oldest son, was that he'd been living in Iaron for the past five years.

King Marcus paused when he saw the captain. "Ah, General Osric. Sorry, it's technically Captain Osric now, isn't it? It *has* been a long time."

"Too long, Your Highness."

"You've done fantastic work here, Captain. All the reports on the Castle Guard have been exemplary. In fact, we've been looking into how to replicate what you've done here in Iaron, Barlin, Velessa, and Treemark."

"I wish you luck, Your Highness."

Torin had to conceal a smile. He knew that tone of Osric's — he didn't believe it. And Torin could understand his skepticism, as Torin himself shared it. The Castle Guard was very much Albin's brainchild, and only had succeeded because of the lord's dedication to the concept. It also helped that Osric was equally dedicated to it, to the point where Albin hadn't really been hands-on the past few years.

The king looked down the line of guards on Osric's left. "These are your lieutenants?"

"Yes, Your Highness," Osric said.

Lady Meerka added, "They are the detectives who solve the more complicated crimes in the demesne."

Osric indicated them with his left hand. "May I present Lieutenants Iaian, Tresyllione, ban Wyvald, Dru, and Grovis."

King Marcus had nodded at Iaian and Danthres, but once Osric introduced Torin, the king's gaze fixed on him, which made him a bit apprehensive.

"So *you're* ban Wyvald."

Swallowing, Torin said, "Ah, yes, Your Highness, I am."

To his right, Torin could see Danthres trying very hard to not smile in glee at Torin's obvious discomfort with being singled out by a monarch.

"I recall you from the war. By name, not by face—you see, shortly after you joined up, we received an official notification from Myverin that you were a fugitive and were to be returned to the Council at once."

"What?" Realizing instantly that the outburst was a breach of protocol, Torin quickly added, "My deepest apologies, Your Highness, I am very—very surprised by your words. I did not realize that the Council had deemed me a fugitive."

"Well, they did." The king actually grinned. "And no need to apologize. It's always nice when someone breaks protocol for a moment. You see the funniest facial expressions that way."

That didn't exactly make Torin feel better. "If I may ask, Your Highness, why did you not fulfill the Council's warrant?"

"Several reasons. I was in the midst of a war, and was reluctant to part with any able-bodied soldiers. I was reliably informed by your commanding officer—" He shot Osric a smiling glance. "—that you were an excellent soldier and an asset to the 17th. And Myverin has no standing army, no military or law-enforcement personnel worth mentioning, and no formal treaties with us, so I didn't really see how they could enforce their request. I see that Myverin never did get you back."

"No, Your Highness. My father attempted a personal appeal for me to return a few months ago, but to no avail."

"His loss is Cliff's End's gain. The demesne is lucky to have you—to have *all* of you." He cast his glance to the other lieutenants. "Now come. Let us go and wish our dear friend Lord Albin well on his way to be with Wiate."

Torin stood back at attention. King Marcus and Queen Marta continued down the hallway, followed by Lady Meerka right behind them. The general from the Royal Guard then turned on his heel and followed behind Lady Meerka on her right, and Osric did likewise at virtually the same time, marching behind the lady on her left.

They continued in that vein, two by two, Royal Guard on the right, Castle Guard on the left, except for the six extra royals, who marched two by two to bring up the rear. Torin found himself marching side by side with one of the two women, a human with hair as red as Torin's own, and eyes as green as the trees. Like the king, she had a misshapen nose, as well as a scar over her left eye that kept that eye half shut. Torin wondered how she dealt with attacks on her left.

Slowly, they marched out through the unusually empty castle corridors. Most everyone was already out in the park, waiting for these final three to arrive. Sir Blayk — Lord Blayk now, Torin thought — was already out on the dais that had been constructed on the far end of Jayka Park, along with the rest of the lord and lady's family, including Blayk's brother, Sir Doval, and his sister, Madam Juliana, and their spouses and children.

Until they came upon the door to the rear balcony, the walk from the office was very quiet, the sound of footfalls echoing in the corridors being the only noise. But as soon as one of the pageboys opened those doors, Torin's ears were assaulted by a cacophony of sound from the park.

The good eye of the woman next to Torin widened and she let out a small gasp when the doors were opened.

The park was packed to the brim with people: humans, elves, dwarves, halflings, and gnomes, all jostling each other and crammed close, and making incredible amounts of noise. Cliff's End was always a loud place, and Torin had experienced some of its most vocal events, from Jorbin's Way during midsummer to the docks at noon when the fishing boats all came in, to the celebrations when it was the birthday of either the lord or the lady.

This had them all beat. Torin saw Danthres in front of him briefly move both hands to her tapered ears, which were far more sensitive due to her elven heritage, before lowering them again quickly.

Around the periphery of the park was a large wooden construction. At the far end was the stage, which included the body of Lord Albin on a table (and surrounded by the blue tinge of a Preservation Spell to keep the body in the same state it was in shortly after Sir Rommett found him a week ago) and a dozen or so chairs, all but three of which were occupied by various members of the nobility, including Sir Rommett, as well as Lady Meerka's surviving family. Standing behind them were two guards and three people holding trumpets.

Radiating outward from that dais around the perimeter of the park was a large catwalk that was the height of three humans, or two and a half elves. Guards in both black and gray were interspersed at regular intervals around the catwalk, and Torin was sure there were plenty in the crowd as well. The catwalk also enabled the king, queen, and lady, as well as their honor guard, to reach the stage from the castle without being mobbed.

His companion's green eyes were going all around the catwalk, so Torin assumed her astonishment was at that rather than the people. Quietly, he said, "The material and time to construct that were donated respectively by the Lumber Guild and the Carpenters Guild."

She turned to glance at Torin with her scarred eye. "Donated? That's unlike a guild."

"Lord Albin was very well loved. Plus, one of his last acts was to approve a change in the tax structure that the guilds had been asking for for months."

The woman shook her head. "Of course."

As soon as the king and queen stepped onto the catwalk, the three trumpeters raised their instruments and blew a fanfare. The crowd suddenly grew quieter, and they all turned around to look up at the king and queen as they walked slowly around the catwalk on the left toward the dais.

As soon as the fanfare ended, someone started applauding, and it spread through the crowd like a fire. The cheers and clapping was even louder than the susurrus of noise that had preceded their arrival, and this time Danthres kept her hands over her ears, protocol be damned.

Torin followed behind Danthres and alongside the red-haired woman all the way down the catwalk to the dais, where Lady Meerka's family were all now standing in deference to royalty. Captain Osric led his people to stand behind the chairs assembled on stage left, while the general and his dozen officers stood behind the chairs on stage right. The king and queen walked past the magickally preserved body of Lord Albin, each pausing for a moment to place a hand on his arm, then walked to their seats.

Once the king and queen sat down, so did everyone else. Torin and the other guards, of course, remained standing.

ALETA LOTHLATHNA STOOD ON THE FAR END OF THE CATWALK, SURVEYING the crowd from her high vantage point with some intensity. The elven woman was working her third straight shift, having volunteered to be on loan to Gryphon Precinct (which covered the region in and around the castle; Aleta normally served in Dragon Precinct, the middle-class district) during her off-time to help in the final preparations for getting Jayka Park ready. The prep work for either hosting the king and queen or a state funeral would be considerable, and that this was both merely compounded the problems.

A bit to her right, one of the Royal Guard made a snorting noise, and said, "I'm impressed, you're not gaping."

Her gaze still being cast over the crowd, Aleta asked, "Gaping at what?"

"Marcus and Marta. Most of the rest of your compatriots are openly staring."

Aleta shrugged. "It's hardly my first time in the presence of royalty."

"Ah, yes, you worked for the Elf Queen, didn't you?"

At that, Aleta finally turned to look at the guard. He had a completely bald head, but a thick beard, and an amused smile. He had the symbol of a shield over the left side of his chest, denoting his rank as that of a lieutenant. "How did you know that?"

He pointed to his neck. "I fought in the war, and I know what that tattoo means."

Frowning, Aleta tugged at the collar of her armor. Usually it covered the neck tattoo of the word in Ra-Telvish for "Shranlaseth," the name of the elven special forces that she had been part of in the Elf Queen's service, before the queen herself disbanded it for reasons neither Aleta nor any of her comrades had ever been able to divine.

She turned to look back at the crowd. "I'm not here to gape, I'm here to make sure everything's secure."

"And is it?"

"No." Aleta indicated the crowd with one hand. "During training, one of the things the *shishook* taught us was that discrepancies are what you should pay attention to."

The lieutenant's tone had gone from friendly and amused to annoyed. "I don't see any discrepancies, I just see everyone cheering at the sight of royalty."

"Not everyone." Aleta hoped for the king and queen's sake that this unobservant idiot wasn't typical of the Royal Guard, though she refrained from saying so out loud. "There's a woman down there who's dealing with a crying infant. There's a couple kissing each other. There are two dwarves arguing with each other. And there are the three halflings who tried to stand on each others' shoulders who fell, and the people around them helping them up. But that's not what concerns me."

"What does?" The guard now sounded concerned.

"Four people." Aleta pointed at each of them, who were interspersed at different spots in the crowd, but all fairly close to the dais. "They're not looking at the king and queen, and they're not being distracted by any of the other things I mentioned. They're looking at each other. All four are regularly maintaining eye contact."

"Mitre's bones," the guard muttered. "I hadn't even noticed that."

While ranks were not completely equivalent between the Castle Guard and the Royal Guard, a lieutenant in the latter still outranked a guard in the former, so Aleta once again held her tongue. Instead, she looked around for one of the runners, guards assigned to take messages back and forth. Finally catching sight of one, she signaled him, and he came running over.

It was Abrik, one of the Gryphon Precinct guards. "What's goin' on, like?"

"There are two humans and two dwarves in the crowd. The humans are both brown-haired, one with a beard and—"

"They're moving!" the lieutenant barked.

Glancing over, Aleta saw that all four of them were trying to push their way closer to the dais. The humans were having less success than the dwarves, who took advantage of their smaller size to weave in and among people. By this time, King Marcus, Queen Marta, and Lady Meerka, as well as the latter's family, had all sat down, and the top-ranking members of the two sets of guards were standing at attention behind them.

Looking back at Abrik, she went on. "The bearded human's wearing a red tunic. The other one's clean-shaven and is wearing a black sleeveless tunic. The two dwarves both have white hair and beards, and one is wearing an eyepatch." Her angle and the dwarves' long hair and beards made it impossible to make out anything beyond that.

Abrik's mouth hung open. "What was the middle part, again, like?"

Aleta snarled, remembering that guards assigned to Gryphon or Unicorn only had to deal with minor nonsense involving the upper classes, so brains weren't always necessary. "Never mind, stay here and take my post. I'll run the message down."

"But—!" Abrik held up a finger, but Aleta was already running down the catwalk toward the side of the dais where Captain Osric and the Castle Guard lieutenants stood. She went around behind them so that she could speak without anyone in the crowd or sitting on the stage noticing.

"Captain, Lieutenants!" she whisper-shouted at their backs.

Both Captain Osric and Lieutenants Iaian and Tresyllione next to him turned around. They were closest to her, and given that the crowd was continuing to cheer and applaud, Aleta wasn't surprised that they were the only ones who heard her.

"What is it?" Osric asked in a similar whisper.

"There are four people in the crowd who I believe have hostile intentions. I'd like to have them removed."

"Based on what?"

Iaian, who'd become friends with Aleta since the incident with Yarbanig, said, "I'd trust her judgment, Cap'n."

Osric shot him a look, then he scowled, rubbing his unusually clean-shaven chin. "Very well. Iaian, Tresyllione, go with her and grab another guard and remove them."

Aleta contained a sigh. She'd been hoping not to have to work with the halfbreed, but she supposed that she couldn't afford to be choosy. Another Gryphon guard, Micah, was positioned nearby where the catwalk met the stage, and Aleta grabbed him.

Quickly, Aleta described the foursome. The dwarf with the eyepatch was already clearly visible pushing his way forward through the crowd.

Tresyllione pointed downstage a bit. "Red tunic?"

Aleta followed her gaze and recognized him, also noticing the other human just to his left. "Yes, and the other human's there." After indicating the human in the black tunic, she moved into the crowd toward the red tunic. She wasn't about to entrust the halfbreed with that.

Pushing her way past people to get to the man, she finally got in sight of him just as he was unsheathing a Thevit dagger.

But as soon as the man caught sight of Aleta, he turned and lost himself quickly in the crowd.

"Damn," Aleta muttered, and shoved aggressively past people.

"'Ey!"

"Watch it, bitch!"

"Why's the Guard bein' all in here?"

Aleta made it halfway through the park before she had to admit that she lost the man completely.

Snarling, she turned and pushed her way back to the side of the dais. En route, she met up with Iaian, and the two of them were able to push through more aggressively.

"I lost one of the dwarves. Micah and Danthres went after the other two."

"Was the dwarf you chased armed?"

Iaian shrugged. "Not that I noticed, but nobody should have weapons in here but us."

"Before I lost mine, I saw him unsheath a Thevit dagger."

"That's a throwin' knife."

Micah was waiting for them at the catwalk. He'd removed his right glove and was inspecting his hand. "The bastard bit me," he said. "Broke skin clear through the damn glove. Gonna need t'see a healer."

"Where's Danthres?" Iaian asked.

"She went after the dwarf."

Aleta's eyes widened. "I didn't even see him."

"He's right here."

Turning, Aleta saw Tresyllione pushing her way rudely through the crowd, gripping the dwarf who had the use of both eyes by the scruff of his neck.

Sir Rommett had gotten up to speak, his voice magickally amplified to be heard by the entire crowd. "Gentle folk, please, if you would quiet down so we may begin this solemn service!"

After glancing up at the stage, Tresyllione looked at Iaian. "He's carrying a throwing knife and a charm of some sort, which I'm willing to bet negates the magick detection our good friends in the Royal Guard put up. I suggest we take this gentleman back to the castle to interrogate him properly. Anything to avoid listening to that shitbrain."

"Sounds good t'me. I had enough with Hawk's funeral last week."

The two lieutenants started to amble up the catwalk. Aleta moved to follow them, but, for the first time, the halfbreed looked at Aleta, who recoiled as if Tresyllione had struck her. The look in her eyes was filled with seething contempt. "*Not* you, Shranlaseth. You go back to standing guard and beating people up and mindlessly killing people. This is *detective* work."

Aleta stood with her mouth hanging open as the two lieutenants continued up the catwalk with the prisoner. *How dare that halfbreed bitch speak down to* me *like that!*

Iaian, at least, had been kind enough to cast back an apologetic glance in her direction. Aleta was too good a soldier to talk back to a higher rank, not even someone as contemptible as Tresyllione, but she had done nothing to earn such ire. She knew the halfbreed could be unpleasant — she'd heard stories from Jared and Simon and from Iaian himself about Tresyllione's attitude problem — but this was well above and beyond that.

With another snarl, she moved more slowly up the catwalk to re-take her post and let Abrik go back to being a runner.

TWO

TORIN YAWNED AS HE ENTERED THE SQUADROOM IN THE EASTERN WING OF THE castle. The previous day had been grueling, as the funeral included eulogies from half the people with the title of "Sir" and "Madam" who lived in the castle, concluding with verbal tributes first from the king, then from the queen, which lasted three-quarters of an hour each. Then the monarchs, Lady Meerka and her family, and the honor guard that Torin was part of all had to go to the body shop, where Lord Albin's body was to be cremated, as per his wishes. (Danthres and Iaian had re-joined the honor guard midway through Queen Marta's speech, the look on the former's face indicating to Torin that the interrogation of their would-be assassin hadn't gone well.)

By the time it all ended, Osric dismissed everyone. Danthres disappeared before Torin had a chance to talk to her, so he just went home and slept.

This morning, he found Sergeant Jonas chatting with Danthres, Iaian, and Dru. Of Osric and Grovis, there was no sign, not in the kitchen nor Osric's office.

"Good morning, all."

"Not so far, it ain't," Dru muttered. "Rommett came in first thing and took the captain and the fish off to talk to Lord Blayk."

Torin frowned. "I can understand wanting to speak to Osric, but Grovis?"

"Who the hell knows?" Dru shrugged. "And honestly, who gives a shit? It's not gonna change anything."

"It might." Iaian had just swallowed a bite from one of the pastries that Jonas always brought from home. "I remember when I was just startin' out, Albin took over from his old man, he started makin' changes right and left, up and down. His kid may do the same thing."

"I don't recall ever meeting Lord Blayk," Torin said. "He wasn't much of a presence even before he moved away."

Danthres finally spoke. "I'm fairly certain I met him a few times, but I'm damned if I can recall anything about him."

"Good," Jonas said emphatically. "If we're lucky, he'll be some bland bureaucrat who will leave everything alone."

Now Danthres stared at the sergeant. "When have we ever been *that* lucky?"

"Speaking of which," Torin said, "how goes it with the dwarf you captured?"

Danthres's habitual sour expression grew more so. "Poorly. He refuses to speak, we have no idea who he is, who his compatriots are, or who hired them."

"One bit'a good news," Iaian said after taking another bite. "We took the charm he was carryin' to Boneen. Like we figured, it's a charm that shields the guy holdin' it from bein' affected by magick. Boneen said it was called a Snavli charm."

Torin nodded. "That explains how they got in."

"Yeah," Jonas said, "the royals were shittin' bricks for a while, 'cause they were worried their detectors weren't workin' right, but we confiscated somethin' like five hundred weapons that the charms *did* pick up."

Danthres shook her head. "Didn't realize that many people had designs on the king and queen."

"Nah, just a buncha folks who thought the no-weapons rules didn't apply to them. And a whole lotta cheap-shit daggers that people from Goblin wear all the time as a matter of course." Jonas chuckled. "Figure sales on personal daggers're gonna spike."

"Anyhow, we stuck him in the hole overnight," Danthres said. "I'll go back at him today."

Iaian popped the last bit of pastry into his mouth. "Good thing Aleta noticed those guys."

Danthres rolled her eyes. "Please. One of us would've noticed them when they approached the stage."

His partner's dismissal surprised Torin. "Danthres, they had Thevits. Those are throwing daggers. They just needed a clear line of sight, and there were four of them. If Aleta hadn't noticed them, we wouldn't have seen anything until the king and queen were dead."

"I doubt that, somehow."

Defensively, Iaian asked, "The hell's your problem with Aleta? She's a damn fine guard, and she used to be Shranlaseth."

"Believe me, Iaian, I'm well aware of that creature's history. I—"

Whatever Danthres was about to say regarding Aleta was cut off by the door to the hallway opening to reveal Lord Blayk, Grovis, and a gnome carrying a slate.

While making a mental note to ask Danthres about her issues with Aleta—Torin agreed with Iaian that she was an excellent guard—Torin found himself wondering where Osric was.

The new lord of the demesne moved to stand in front of Osric's office, the gnome following and standing to his right. Blayk was tall and long-necked, but also very wiry, excepting the small potbelly he carried in the middle. His hairline had receded, and he was likely to wind up as bald as his father before too long. Also like his father, he sported a thick mustache.

Grovis meekly walked to his own desk and sat at it. The young detective carried a stunned visage, much the same way he looked when he found out that his cousin's fiancée was killed.

"Lieutenants, Sergeant, I am Lord Blayk, as I am sure you are aware. I understand that one of your comrades died around the same time as my father, and I would like to offer my condolences on that."

Jonas opened his mouth as if to thank Blayk, but the lord continued before he had a chance.

"Whilst I appreciate how difficult this transition must be, I feel that it is important to take a good hard look at how things are done, and change them where appropriate. My father was a great man, but I believe he grew unnecessarily complacent as the years went on. He also had a bit of a tendency toward sentiment over practicality. To that end, there are many changes I wish to make in the structure of the city-state, including that of the Castle Guard. I believe the work my father did in repurposing the Guard has been impressive, but misguided in some ways. For example, he had a tendency to romanticize the elven war. While I am sure Osric served the king and queen admirably in that conflict, I believe that it would be more appropriate for a man of breeding to be in charge of so important an institution as the Castle Guard."

Torin started getting a queasy feeling in his stomach. Bad enough he was so dismissive of the elven war, in which Torin had fought, and of Osric, under whom he'd served. But his final words also indicated a decision that would anger just about everyone in the squadroom, if not in the entirety of the Guard, and which he also suspected was the reason for the look on Grovis's face.

"To that end, I have offered Osric retirement, with full twenty-five-year benefits."

Iaian tensed. He had, Torin knew, been counting the minutes until his own twenty-five-year pension vested, and having eleven-year veteran Osric be given that without having to wait another decade and a half didn't appear to sit well.

"He has accepted, and I have promoted Amilar Grovis to be your new captain and the head of the Guard. Is there something you wish to say, Lieutenant Tresyllione?"

Looking over at his partner, Torin saw that Danthres—who had been leaning casually against a desk—was now standing upright, hands on hips. "I actually have several thi—"

"Keep them to yourself, please, Lieutenant, I have a very long day ahead of me, and the purpose of this meeting is for you to be briefed, not for you to register complaints over decisions that have already been made and will not be changing." Blayk tugged on one end of his mustache and then turned to Iaian. "Lieutenant, I am told that you are only two years from vesting your own twenty-five-year pension, yes?"

"Uh, yeah—yeah, I am."

"No longer. I believe that the Guard needs an infusion of youth. Your service to the Guard has been exemplary, and I would say that you have earned the opportunity to retire early rather than wait out an arbitrary number. Therefore, I am making you the same offer I made to Osric. If you choose to retire now, you will retain the full benefits of a twenty-five year veteran. What say you?"

Iaian's mouth was now hanging open in much the same way Grovis's did, which amused Torin no end. "I say shit yeah, my lord."

Blayk pursed his lips. "A simple yes would suffice, Lieutenant. Very well, see Sir Rommett after we are concluded here and he shall provide you with the same paperwork he is currently providing for Osric."

"Absolutely, my lord." Iaian was actually grinning. Torin had known Iaian for a decade, and he was quite sure he'd never seen quite so giddy an expression on the old man's face.

"That leaves three openings in your squad." Blayk held out a hand, and the gnome silently handed the slate to him. "Sir Rommett informs me that the next two guards up for promotion are Arn Kellan, currently assigned to Goblin Precinct, and Manfred, currently assigned to Dragon

Precinct. So they will take the positions vacated by Lieutenant Iaian's retirement and Captain Grovis's promotion."

Torin shook his head. There was just something wrong sounding about "Captain Grovis."

"Lieutenant Hawk will also need to be replaced, and to that end, I am promoting a guard assigned to Dragon Precinct named Aleta lothLathna."

"What!?" Danthres cried out, which prompted another angry look from Blayk.

However, Blayk's next words were less angry than his last at Danthres. "For what it is worth, Lieutenant, she would not have been my first choice, either, but King Marcus and Queen Marta were extremely grateful to her for her efforts in stopping the would-be assassins, and when told that she was still only a guard, they were insistent upon her being promoted to detective."

Danthres let out a very long breath and nodded. Even she wasn't foolish enough to argue with the king and queen.

"Furthermore, she will be partnered with Lieutenant Dru, and they shall take over the investigation into the assassination attempt."

That revelation trumped Danthres's self-control, as she blurted out, "That's *my* case!" Technically, it was hers and Iaian's, but given that Iaian was now sitting at his desk with a massive goofy grin on his face at having achieved two of his fondest desires in one shot—no longer being partnered with Grovis and retiring with a full pension—nothing could truly be called to be his case anymore.

"Again, Lieutenant Tresyllione, this is a royal mandate. Unless you wish to be partnered with h—"

"No!" Danthres barked. "She can have the case."

"Good." Blayk handed the slate back to the gnome. "Now then, I have spent a goodly amount of time the past week going over the various files on your cases. I have observed that Lieutenants Tresyllione and ban Wyvald have the best records in the squadroom, and to that end, I feel it would be in the best interests of improving the Guard's record if you were split up."

Only the fact that Blayk had made it clear what he thought of interruptions prevented Torin from speaking up to point out the logical fallacy in that statement. He and Danthres closed cases because they worked well *together*. And Torin was the only person who'd proved able to work with Danthres at all. Torin was the seventh partner she'd had in half a year's time when he joined up a decade ago, and had Torin not worked out, she would've been fired.

"Therefore," Blayk continued, "Lieutenant Kellan will partner with Lieutenant Tresyllione, and Lieutenant Manfred will pair up with Lieutenant ban Wyvald. And, of course, Lieutenants Dru and lothLathna are partners as well." The lord took a deep breath and clapped his hands together suddenly, startling Torin as the echo of the clap reverberated throughout the squadroom. "I believe that—"

"Excuse me, m'lord!"

Turning, Torin saw one of the castle pageboys standing in the doorway.

"I'm sorry t'interrupt, m'lord, but Lady Meerka's askin' to see Lieutenants Tresyllione an' ban Wivvy."

Chuckling, Torin said, "Well, at least he got one of our names right."

Blayk testily asked, "What does my mother wish to see *these* two for?"

Torin and Danthres exchanged glances, Torin trying to say, *Don't say anything!* with his expression, and Danthres using hers to reluctantly agree. She also seemed intrigued by the lady of the demesne wishing to see them.

"I couldn't say, your lordship, but her ladyship made it clear that I wasn't to be comin' back without the two lieutenants, your lordship, sir."

"We shall go together, then," Blayk said. "Come along."

He led the gnome out. Torin and Danthres exchanged another set of glances and then followed.

The last thing Torin heard when leaving the squadroom was Iaian saying, "This is the best day of my shit-ass life!"

THREE

Danthres was having difficulty processing things today.

First Hawk died in the line of duty. Danthres had always found Hawk to be a decent detective and a decent person, but if he had to die, at least he did it while doing his job. There were worse ways to go, and Danthres had seen most of them, going back to the mass grave of infant halfbreeds she found in Bronnwick years ago.

Lord Albin's death was as great a shock as Hawk's. Sure, the lord of the demesne had been ill, but he was always ill at this time of the year. It was as reliable as the time chimes.

And now Albin's idiot son was making changes, each one stupider than the last. She would not miss Iaian, as she'd hated the old bastard since her days as a guard in Goblin, but making Osric retire? And putting that fish-faced shitbrain *Grovis* in charge?

Ever since being forced out of Sorlin, Danthres had struggled to find a place for herself, failing to do so in Bronnwick or in Treemark. It took a while to settle into Cliff's End, but she'd made a life here as a lieutenant, as Torin's partner, and as Osric's subordinate. Now only one of those things was true, and she didn't like it one single bit.

Of course, it could have been worse. Blayk could have paired her up with Manfred. That would have been cause for resigning right then and there.

Well, perhaps it wouldn't be *that* bad, and she knew this day would come eventually, since Manfred was next up on the promotion list. But she certainly wasn't looking forward to being in the same squadroom with him.

Or with Aleta. She shuddered at the damage that Shranlaseth bitch could do as a lieutenant.

Now, though, she followed Torin and Blayk and his quiet little gnome to the lady's offices. Danthres had never been to that particular room before, indeed had seen very little of Lady Meerka. What few dealings she had with the nobility were with Sir Rommett, and before him Sir Gevlin, and very occasionally with Lord Albin. That they were so few was a testament, she felt, to Osric's leadership.

Lady Meerka was sitting behind a desk that was covered in neat piles of parchment, plus a few rolled-up scrolls, which were also neatly piled on one side of the desk. She looked up from the one scroll she was studying and frowned. "What are you doing here, Blayk? I wished to see Lieutenants Tresyllione and ban Wyvald. I didn't summon you."

Using a tone that was closer to that of a parent with a recalcitrant child than the other way around, Blayk said, "Mother, *I'm* now in charge of the Castle Guard. If there's something you wish to speak to the lieutenants about, you should do it through me."

"That's a complete waste of time, Blayk. I'm perfectly capable of speaking to them on my own." She let out a sigh that caused a whistle between her teeth. "Then again, this does concern your father, so I suppose it makes sense for you to be here."

"Why in Wiate's name would you want to talk to them about *Father*?"

Danthres shifted uncomfortably back and forth on her feet. The last thing she wanted to listen to was an argument between these two.

"That is a ridiculous question to ask, Blayk, as I have not had a chance to explain my summons. If you'd simply be patient, I will answer your question. Indeed, if you had not spoken, your question would have been answered in any event. You're always doing this, asking unnecessary questions."

Blayk actually rolled his eyes at that. Danthres glanced over at Torin, who was maintaining his polite visage, but she could determine the slightest twitch of his lips under his thick red beard.

There were no guest chairs in the lady's office, so the four of them were forced to stand. Meerka did not rise, however, so Danthres found herself staring mostly at her red curls.

"According to the laws of the demesne, in particular a law that was very important to Albin, whenever someone dies in Cliff's End in a manner that may not be natural, it is to be investigated by the lieutenants of the Castle Guard."

"What does this have to do with Father?" Blayk asked snidely.

Meerka closed her eyes and did the teeth-whistling sigh again. "I believe I just mentioned how impatient you are, Blayk? Please, allow me to finish what I intend to say to these two detectives, and your questions *will* be answered."

Blayk made a *go on* gesture.

"At first, we all believed that my husband died of natural causes. He had been ill for some time with his usual late-summer malady, though it was noticeably worse this time. In fact, I had sent for my son to come back to Cliff's End the day before he died."

Danthres whirled to look at Blayk, who hadn't changed his expression. She barely managed to scrape together enough decorum to not comment, but still, this was something she hadn't known before.

"However, this morning was the first time my husband's sitting room was tidied up since Sir Rommett found his body. Blayk has preferred to use Albin's former office, and apparently the house faerie was waiting for someone to tell her to clean the sitting room, which doesn't make any sense, as the house faerie is supposed to clean it every evening."

Now Danthres did speak up. "Actually, my lady, that was our fault."

Meerka blinked. "I wasn't aware that you interacted with the house faerie."

"We didn't, my lady," Torin said, "but we instructed one of the servants to do so. After Sir Rommett informed us of your husband's death, we went to his sitting room to investigate. We told a nearby servant—I'm afraid we never got his name—to instruct the house faerie to not clean the room until she received further instructions."

Danthres continued: "However, Sir Rommett later told us that we wouldn't be investigating Lord Albin's death. Unfortunately, I guess that nobody shared that with the house faerie."

"Ah. Well, that makes sense, at least." Meerka nodded firmly. "It is fortuitous that you mentioned that you were intending to investigate my husband's death, for that is what I wish you to do now."

"Mother, I'm sorry," Blayk said in as unapologetic a tone as it was possible to have, "but Father died of his illness."

"I'm not so sure of that. You see, the house faerie discovered that the mug from which Albin drank water and wine was poisoned."

Danthres started. "Was she sure?"

"Of course she was," Meerka said as if the question was ridiculous.

Torin was nodding in agreement. "Many of the fae are able to detect poisons. They're also immune to them, thankfully."

"Very thankfully, as she drank what little was left in the mug—that was when she detected the poison."

Danthres recalled that the mug was full when they found the body, but that *was* a week ago . . .

"I realize," Meerka went on, "that Albin's body has already been burned and that you therefore cannot examine it to determine for sure that he was killed by the poison in his drink, but it seems to at least be probable that he was—or, at the very least, possible. That possibility is enough for the law to apply and an investigation to commence."

Blayk was shaking his head. "Mother, this is ridiculous. There's no one in Cliff's End who wanted Father dead. You saw the funeral yesterday. Everyone loved him here."

Meerka regarded her son witheringly. "I dare say we could find one person who did not love him, thus disproving your hypothesis, Blayk. And indeed it would only take one person to kill him, if they had access to poison." She turned her gaze back to Danthres and Torin. "My husband spoke very highly of the two of you, particularly after that incident with the Hamnau gem. I also recall being relieved that it was the two of you who were handling Gan Brightblade's murder. Therefore, I wish it to be the pair of you who investigate the death of my husband."

Danthres started to say, "It will be an hono—"

She was cut off by Blayk, who stepped forward. "Mother, this isn't possible. As I told you, the Castle Guard is in *my* purview now, and Lieutenants ban Wyvald and Tresyllione are no longer partners."

Pursing her lips, Meerka said, "That doesn't make any sense. They have the best arrest record in the Guard."

"Which is why I split them up," Blayk said slowly. "Their acumen will be on twice the cases now."

"Oh, very well." Meerka threw up her hands and got to her feet. "As long as at least one of them investigates with whomever he or she is paired with, that will be satisfactory. But the law is *very* clear on this, and I'm only sorry we didn't learn of the exigent circumstances until after Albin's body was destroyed."

"Mother, I don't think—"

"You're right, Blayk, you don't think. I am the lady of the demesne. You know I prefer not to lord my title over others, as I find it tedious, but I will do so if I must. I have as much right to insist on an investigation as you do. In fact, it is the same right. Furthermore, if someone *did* kill your father, I would think you'd want to know who it was. Someone poisoning the leader of the most populous city-state in Flingaria is something I believe should be punished — and you should believe that, too."

"If I *believed* that he *was* killed, I would be the first to insist upon the Guard looking into it." He let out a long sigh and turned to Danthres. "But very well, if you insist. Lieutenant Tresyllione, you've been paired with Lieutenant Kellan, I believe?"

The gnome nodded assent, as did Danthres.

Turning back to Meerka, Blayk said, "I'll have them open a case file as soon as Kellan settles in, if that's acceptable to you, Mother?"

Meerka folded her hands on the desk. "It is, yes." She looked up at Danthres. "Lieutenant, I will instruct everyone in the castle to cooperate with you fully. If Lord Albin was killed, the ramifications will be almost incalculable. You may all leave now, I have a great deal of work to do."

Danthres was surprised at the abruptness of the dismissal, but she was more than happy to accept it. She and Torin left the room quickly, followed by Blayk and his gnome.

They got most of the way down the corridor, and were about to turn right toward the eastern wing, when Blayk said, "Lieutenant Tresyllione, a word."

Closing her eyes, Danthres stopped and turned to face the young man. Torin, to her relief, also stopped, standing just a short distance away for support. "Yes, my lord?"

"I do not wish to offend my mother, but obviously she is blinded by grief. Father died of an illness."

"The house faerie's — "

Blayk stared at her. "I'm not going to accuse someone of murdering one of the most popular leaders in the human lands on the word of a *house faeire*. They're hardly reliable."

"Actually," Torin said, "house fae have been extremely useful in solving several cases over the years."

"Nevertheless, this is a fool's errand," Blayk said tartly to Torin, then regarded Danthres with a stern expression. "Lieutneant Tresyllione, I want you to at least do a perfunctory investigation, which should be enough to satisfy my mother, but leave it at that."

With that, he turned and walked straight down the corridor, the gnome following as quickly behind as his little legs would carry him.

Danthres stared at her now-former partner. "Quite a morning."

"Indeed." He turned to continue down the corridor, Danthres's long strides quickly catching up with him.

"Remember what I said to you after Osric first partnered us up?" Danthres asked.

Torin grinned. "That I would have a tenure as your partner as short as that of my predecessors."

With a sigh, Danthres said, "I suppose, then, that we should both be grateful that we got ten years out of it."

"I'm certainly grateful, Danthres. And I must admit, I'm looking forward to the challenge of seeing if Manfred—not to mention Kellan and Aleta—can be good detectives."

"I'm sure they won't," Danthres said dismissively. "The only one who has a chance is Manfred, and that's because he's paired up with you. I think I taught you enough that you'll make a good trainer."

Chuckling, Torin said, "I was just going to say that I taught you enough that you'll do likewise for Kellan."

"Well, we'll find out, won't we?" They reached the vestibule, the very same spot where Sir Rommett had informed them of Lord Albin's death a week ago. "This investigation will certainly be a challenge."

Torin rolled his eyes. "What, the perfunctory investigation into the meaningless death of Lord Albin?"

Danthres let out a derisive snort. "Hardly. I plan to work this case the same as any other. No matter what Lord Blayk says. Hell, I wanted to make it a proper case in the first place, and now that she's given us an in? I'm for damn sure taking it."

FOUR

Dru stood in the interview room, barely able to work up the energy to remember who it was they were talking to.

Looking over at the cracked and pitted wooden table, he saw a dwarf sitting unusually calmly on the stool on the other side of it, hands folded on its surface. In one of the two chairs facing it was Aleta, her earth-colored cloak still new and creased in spots.

Dru himself was leaning against the wall of the deliberately poorly lit room, but all he could think about was the way the argument he had with his wife Zan ended this morning. He couldn't even remember what the argument was about or how it started, but they'd gone at it pretty nastily, and it concluded with Zan lamenting Dru's inability to understand what she wanted, and Dru saying, "Well, then maybe you should find a husband who does," and leaving.

That was a stupid-ass way to leave the house. That thought had been running through his head all morning.

"Look," Aleta was saying to the dwarf, "the longer you try to hold out, the worse it's going to be. You and your comrades tried to kill the king and queen. That isn't something that is likely to end well for you."

The dwarf just shrugged, and unfolded his hands, palms up on the table.

Aleta, Dru noticed, was staring at the dwarf's hands for some reason. Then she looked up at his face. "We've been at this an hour, and since you're too stupid to try to explain why you smuggled a throwing knife into a gathering led by the king and queen—which, by the way, will *all by itself* get you fifty years on the barge—we're just going to throw you back in the hole." She got to her feet. "Maybe another night down there will convince you to talk."

One of the guards assigned to the castle, Yorn Bonce, was standing outside. "You get anything?" he asked.

Dru shook his head. "Shitbrain ain't sayin' nothin'. Haul his ass back to the hole, will ya, Bonce?"

"Sure, Lieutenant. And hey, Aleta, congratulations on the promotion."

Aleta didn't say anything at first, then shook her head. "Hm? Oh, thanks Yorn." She then went to sit at her new desk. Dru tried not to wince and failed. He didn't like seeing anyone other than Hawk sitting there. She stared at the dwarf as Bonce led him out of the interview room and then out of the squadroom. Once they were gone, she glanced up at Dru. "Did you notice his hands?"

"What?" Dru blinked twice. "Who gives a shit what his hands look like? In fact, who *gives* a shit, *period*?"

That made Aleta recoil, making her look a lot like Zan had earlier.

Quickly Dru said, "Sorry, but look, it's not like anything happened. Everyone's got their tights in a bunch 'cause someone thought about killin' the king and queen. Know what? People think about that shit all 'a time! For the last week it ain't been nothin' but Lord Albin's dead, and someone tried to kill the king and queen. My partner's dead, and nobody seems to even *care*!"

Looking around, Dru saw that there was nobody else in the squadroom, and he breathed a sigh of relief. His words had echoed off the walls, and if Sergeant Jonas or any of the other detectives or Grovis (Dru refused to think of him as *Captain* Grovis—that was just wrong in every possible way) had been there, it would've been beyond embarrassing.

Aleta gave him a sympathetic look. "I'm sorry about your partner— truly, he was a good person. And I'm especially sorry that my promotion was due in part to his death. But we do have a case here. You saw him, I threatened him with fifty years on the barge, and he didn't even blink. Plus, his clothes were pretty ordinary cotton and linen—the type of stuff you can get by the yard on the discount tables down Jorbin's Way. How does someone like that afford a charm that can get past the Royal Guard's magick?"

For the first time, Dru looked at Aleta as something other than Hawk's replacement. "Okay, those're good points."

"Here's a better one. His hands had old scars on them that looked to me like rope burns. Specifically the type of rope burns that sailors get. I used to see them all the time in the Shranlaseth." She got to her feet. "I suggest we get a crystal with his image from the magickal examiner and spend the rest of the day at the docks showing it around and seeing who recognizes him."

Dru let out a breath. "Why the hell'd we do that?"

"I just said, he was a sailor once."

"No, you said he *might've* been a sailor once, and it ain't like the dockrats're big on talkin' to anybody wearin' armor."

She put her hands on her hips. "You have a better idea?"

Hesitating, Dru just stared at her for a second. "Look, I get that you're all excited an' shit, but don't go gettin' your hopes up, all right?"

Frowning, Aleta asked, "What do you mean?"

He just chuckled and shook his head. "I remember my first day onna job after I got promoted. It was just like with you, only it was two guys needed replacing 'stead'a three. A couple partners, just like me an' Hawk were, they got into a nasty spot. Walked into the wrong building. They were goin' in there to talk to someone about a case, they accidentally walked in on a contract killin'. They stopped it, an' the guys who did it got caught and the magistrate hung their asses. But Nael was killed, an' Karistan lost her arm. See, if you're lucky, you make it through your life makin' a tiny amount'a difference, but mostly? We're trash collectors. We find the trash, we dump it in the hole, and then we go find new trash. An' at the end of it, nobody gives a shit, an' nobody gets outta here in one piece. You either die or you get hurt."

"Or you retire. Captain Osric and Lieutenant Iaian both seem to be getting out in one piece."

Dru snorted. "If you think they're in one piece, then you ain't payin' attention." He waved a hand at her dismissively. "Look, you wanna go to the docks, go ahead."

Aleta started toward the door, then stopped when she realized that Dru wasn't following her. "Are you coming with me?"

"Why should I?'

"Because you're the senior partner in this case." She again put her hands on her hips. "And because I'm still new at this and could use your guidance."

He pointed at her. "That hands-on-hips thing, that somethin' they teach you in the Shranlaseth to scare people with?"

"Are you coming or not?"

Hauling himself to his feet, Dru said, "Fine, I'm comin'. I just hope the boat Hawk was buyin' ain't still in dock."

Aleta nodded. "Right, I remember you mentioning that at the funeral service."

Dru sighed. "Yeah. Let's go, already."

First, they had to go down to Boneen's lair. The magickal examiner's sanctum was a room on the lower floor of the castle that was only accessible via a door at the bottom of a staircase. Mercifully, the door was open; Dru still had nightmares from the Corvin case, when he and Hawk had to deal with the screeching animated door-knocker and the irritating sprite minding the place while Boneen was away at a meeting with the Brotherhood of Wizards.

The diminutive wizard was waddling across to one of the shelves that contained various scrolls, jars, gems, herbs, and other items organized in no obvious manner.

"Hey, Boneen, we need a crystal."

Turning, Boneen regarded both of them with annoyance. "Excuse me? A crystal? Wonderful. Why is it every time I'm in the midst of taking a lovely nap, one of you imbeciles with brown cloaks has to come in and interrupt?"

"With respect, sir," Aleta said with far more deference than Dru had ever felt that Boneen deserved, "you were not asleep when we entered."

"Are you contradicting me, lothLathna?"

"Of course not!" Aleta said quickly, actually taking a step backward.

Dru couldn't help but smile. Being deferential to Boneen was pointless, as he wasn't impressed by it. Generally, the best way to deal with his vitriol was to give as good as you got. Aleta's approach would just prompt Boneen to focus all of his considerable obnoxiousness on her. Which suited Dru fine, as it meant he could sit and watch.

"Are you two looking for any crystal or —"

"We were told that you had an image of the dwarf we have in custody."

"What, the one involved in the conspiracy to assassinate the king and queen?"

Dru started to say, "Yeah, that one," but Aleta spoke first.

"Actually, we don't know that for sure. Strictly speaking, we only are able to hold him for smuggling a weapon into Jayka Park. We don't know for sure that the king and queen were the targets, though that is the obvious choice. But he refuses to speak, or even identify himself, so we need to find out who he is in order for us to—"

Boneen held up a hand. "A simple 'yes' would have sufficed, lothLathna." He turned to Dru. "Does she always blather on this much?"

"Dunno, she's only been my partner for a day."

"I prefer your late, lamented friend Hawk. He at least knew when to be quiet." That last was punctuated by a fierce glare at Aleta, who again took a step back.

Then the M.E. turned to the shelves. "In any event, I do have that crystal. Let me just find it, here. Ah!" He grabbed a crystal and handed it to Dru.

He gripped the crystal with both hands and concentrated, at which point an image of Lord Albin appeared over it. "Uh, Boneen?"

Muttering a curse, the wizard snatched the crystal out of Dru's hand. "These blessed things look too much alike. If this idiot elf hadn't been distracting me with her tiresome minutiae about your idiotic procedure..." He grabbed another crystal and practically shoved it in Dru's face. "Here."

Again Dru gripped the crystal and concentrated. Again an image appeared. Again it wasn't a dwarf—this time it was a halfling. "Pretty sure that's the suspect Iaian and Grovis picked up in that assault case a couple days ago," Dru said with a grin.

"Dammit!"

Boneen provided several crystals in succession, which provided images of Gan Brightblade, the weapon used in the triple murder Dru and Hawk had solved just prior to midsummer, and the Hamnau gem that had been the center of that crazy case Torin and Danthres had had a few months back, before finally getting the right one.

Relieved at the sight of the same face hovering over the crystal that he had just seen a few minutes before in the interview room, Dru thanked Boneen for his help.

"Don't mention it, Dru. I mean that sincerely, I would prefer never to be reminded of this encounter again."

As the two detectives beat a hasty retreat upstairs, Aleta said, "I've never dealt with the M.E. directly before. I've seen him at crime scenes and such, but I've never had to interact with him one-on-one. Is he *always* like that?"

"Nah," Dru said, "usually he's disagreeable."

"Wonderful," Aleta muttered.

They left the castle and walked in companionable silence down Meerka Way through the tree-lined thoroughfares of Unicorn Precinct, the upper-class district. Dru found himself enjoying the silence.

"This is very bizarre," Aleta said suddenly, startling Dru out of his reverie. Upon seeing this, she added, "I'm sorry, I didn't mean to startle you."

"S'okay." He shook his head. "Always like walkin' through Unicorn. It's all quiet. Lets you think."

"What were you thinking about?"

Dru hesitated. "Actually, I wasn't thinkin' about anything. Was kinda nice."

"Well, whatever thoughts you weren't lost in had to have been pretty intense. We're not in Unicorn anymore, we're in Dragon."

Frowning, Dru looked around and realized that they were now surrounded by smaller structures, more shops, and there were actually people wandering around, meaning they were in the middle-class section of Dragon Precinct. "Didn't even realize we'd passed Oak Way. Usually gets louder when you come into Dragon."

"I know — that's what I was talking about. I've been in the Guard for seven years, the last four and a half working Dragon. I've never heard it as quiet as it's been the past week. I thought with the funeral it might pick up, but apparently not."

When they crossed Axe Lane into Goblin Precinct, the slums of the city-state, the quiet remained. There were more people on the street than in Dragon, but fewer than usual. And they all avoided even making eye contact with Aleta or Dru.

"I was talking with a friend of mine who serves in Goblin," Aleta said as one person caught sight of the pair of them and ran into an alleyway, looking frightened. "Crime is lower than it's been in Goblin at any time that wasn't midwinter."

Dru nodded. "Good. With all the people gettin' over their Bliss addiction, an' the shitbrains who killed Hawk bein' from Goblin, they better hide."

After crossing the River Walk, they were in the docklands, which was covered by Mermaid Precinct. It was past midday, so most of the fishing ships had returned from their morning runs and their daily catches had been offloaded. The air had the distinct tinge of fish about it.

To Dru's complete lack of surprise, they spent the next hour and a half showing the dwarf's image to dozens of people on the docks, none of whom recognized him.

"I'm starving," Dru said after they finished talking to Jann Forlis, the first mate of the *Esmerelda*. "Let's get some food. I toldja this was a waste of time."

"The ship he served on may not be in dock." Aleta's optimism was something Dru found almost endearing.

"Or one of the shitbrains we just talked to was lyin' through his teeth. You ever work Mermaid?"

Aleta shook her head as they approached the Dancing Seagull. "No. I started out in Unicorn for half a year, then was in Goblin for a year before going to Dragon."

Dru's eyes widened as he opened the door. "You worked Goblin after only six months?"

She smiled. "The night shift, too. Which was mostly breaking up brawls—not the use I expected my Shranlaseth training to go toward when I joined."

"Yeah, I bet."

They took a seat at a booth. "I got transferred after I broke up a brawl in the Ogre's Breath. I was off-duty at the time, meeting friends for drinks, and some idiot dwarf got into it with a random dumb human."

"Yeah, that's every night at the OB."

"I kept the injuries to a minimum, and Sergeant Markon requested my transfer."

A figure walked over to them. Dru saw the person's shadow first, and was about to ask for a drink when he saw that it wasn't a waiter, but rather another member of the Guard, sporting a green cloak indicating the rank of sergeant.

Looking up, he smiled. "Hey, Mannit. Sorry, *Sergeant* Mannit."

"Dru. Sorry, *Lieutenant* Dru. Still can't believe you outrank me, you stupid shitbrain." The smile falling from his face, Mannit asked, "How are you holding up?"

"Some days suck slightly less than others. Oh hey, this is who they saddled me with now that Hawk's gone. Aleta lothLathna, this is Sergeant Mannit."

Aleta smiled. "It's good to see you again, Sergeant. I'd heard Captain Osric talked you out of retirement."

"Yeah, and now they're tryin' to talk me back into it. Crazy-ass world."

"You two know each other?" Dru asked, not entirely surprised. Mannit was a Guard lifer who knew *everybody*.

"She got assigned to Dragon about a month before I got my twenty-five," Mannit said. "Saved my ass during the Troll Riots."

Dru looked upon Aleta with respect. Mannit had only told Dru that a fellow guard saved him from being pummeled by one of the trolls. He had retired shortly after that, only to be pressed back into service just before midsummer when the previous sergeant in charge of Mermaid, Gaffni, had been forced to resign following a scandal. "That was her?"

Aleta looked away briefly. "Trolls are relatively simple to deal with if you know the trick of it."

Mannit chuckled. "Need you to teach me that trick one'a these days."

Dru gave the sergeant a sidelong glance. "Who's tryin'a talk you *back* into retirement?"

"New lord." Mannit shrugged. "Offered me a full pension again, even though I already got one. I turned 'em down. Now that I'm committed again, I'm for damn sure committed. So what brings you detectives down to my little corner of Cliff's End?"

"Tryin' t'identify a suspect." Dru nodded to Aleta.

She removed the crystal from her pack. Dru had been using it at first, but it took effort to make it function, and after the first four interviews, not to mention all the false alarms in Boneen's lair, Dru was getting seriously fatigued. So he handed it over to Aleta, who had shown no signs of that fatigue even after twice as many uses of the crystal.

As soon as Aleta projected the image, Mannit nodded. "I know this shitbrain. Used t'be second mate on the *Esmerelda*. Was a sailor about ten years back, an' was second mate up until a year ago. Don't remember his name, but if you ask Zaile or Forlis, they'll remember."

Dru stared at Aleta, who looked furious. "Didn't I tell you?"

Aleta snarled, and Dru actually flinched at the new harshness in her visage. "I need to speak to Forlis again."

"When you do," Mannit said, "mention the unlicensed magick he's got crated up below decks in the boxes marked as fruit."

Now Aleta turned her unpleasant gaze upon Mannit—who, Dru noticed, did not flinch. "If he has contraband on his boat, why haven't you seized it?"

"What for?" Mannit pursed his lips. "That shit's the Brotherhood's lookout, not mine. I seize it, I gotta deal with wizards for a week jumpin' through their hoops. No thanks. 'Sides, it's better t'hold onto somethin' like that for when you need it—like when you catch 'em lyin' about a suspect who tried t'kill the king an' queen."

"Good point." Aleta rose and strode purposefully toward the door.

"What about lunch?" Dru called out after her.

Mannit looked down at him. "Last time I saw that look on her face, she was standin' over a dead troll one minute later."

After letting out a long breath, Dru hauled himself to his feet. "All right, but I'd better damn well get lunch after this."

He went back out onto the docks, Mannit's laughter fading behind him as he moved quickly to catch up to Aleta, heading back toward the *Esmerelda*.

Forlis was talking with one of his sailors when he noted the approach of the two detectives. "Look, Lieutenants, I done toldja, I ain't never seen that dwarf before. I got me some *business* here I gotta be takin' care of, an' I can't be doin' that if'n you lot're interruptin' my day."

"Really?" Aleta put a lot of anger into that one word. "Because we have it on good authority that he was second mate on your boat until very recently."

The sailor with Forlis said, "What, Gobink?"

Forlis whipped his hand out as if to backhand the sailor across the face. But Aleta grabbed Forlis's wrist. She was sufficiently fast that Dru never actually saw her make the move—one moment she was facing Forlis, the next she had his wrist.

"'Ey!" Forlis cried. "Let go'a me!"

"I don't think so, Mr. Forlis. You see, had I not grabbed your wrist just now, Lieutenant Dru and I would have had to add assault to the charges that are piling up against you right now."

"Look, I don't know what you're on about, Lieutenant, but—"

Again, Dru saw no actual movement. But suddenly Aleta had twisted Forlis's arm behind the first mate's back. The sailor, wisely, chose that moment to run away very fast.

"Nnnnnnngggggggh!" was the only noise Forlis could manage, his face now contorted into a rictus of pain.

"First of all, we can charge you with smuggling unlicensed magick in those crates you've labeled as fruit. That, by the way, will require you to be questioned, not by me, but by the Brotherhood of Wizards who, if they dislike your answer, are likely to transform you into one of the fruits your manifest claims is in those crates. Second of all, we can charge you with obstructing our investigation into the assassination attempt on the king and queen at Lord Albin's funeral. The magistrate will likely not be impressed by whatever feeble defense you muster up regarding loyalty to past shipmates."

With that, Aleta let go of Forlis's arm and threw him to the dock.

Gripping his shoulder as he lay sprawled on the wooden dock, Forlis stared up past his shoulder at Aleta. "For shit's sake, lady, whyn'tcha tell me this was about the king and queen? Woulda toldja right off."

Dru stepped forward, suddenly feeling the need to contribute. "Then start telling, Forlis, or she'll finish the job an' rip the arm out."

Forlis struggled to his feet. Neither Dru nor Aleta made a move to help him, so he did so slowly and awkwardly. "Look, Gobink was a good sailor. Cap'n was makin' him second mate for good reason. He was turnin' us onto some good clients over the years. But then he up an' quit a year ago for no reason. Didn't nobody see hide nor hair of him—till a few months back. He showed up on Saptor Isle with a bunch of other folks."

"What kinda folks?" Dru asked.

"'Nother dwarf, 'cept that one was havin' an eyepatch, an' two humans, one bare-cheeked, one not."

Aleta looked at Dru. "Our other three would-be assassins."

Dru nodded and looked back at Forlis. "What'd they do in Saptor?"

"Booked passage, they did. Paid extra coin for the good bunks, and paid even more coin for folks to be stayin' quiet. S'why I didn't tell you before, I got me a heavy money purse thanks to him in exchange for keepin' my lips tight. But I didn't know there was no political shit. I ain't havin' no truck with that, an' neither's the cap'n. That's just bad for business, *that* is."

"Can you tell us anything else about Gobink?" Aleta asked.

Forlis finally stopped massaging his shoulder. "Yeah, he got himself a wife an' three kids up in dwarf country — somewhere in the Zignat Mountains, I think."

Aleta looked at Dru, who nodded, grateful that she gave him the consideration. In truth, his own contributions were all but meaningless, which he found annoying. *Maybe if I got my damn head into it, I'd be able to keep up.*

"Thank you for your cooperation," Aleta said, and she and Dru both turned to leave.

"Hey, that mean you ain't tellin' the Brotherhood 'bout the, ah — the fruit?"

Aleta looked back over her shoulder and smiled sweetly. "We'll see, won't we?"

Dru chuckled. "Nice. Now let's celebrate by gettin' lunch."

"Shouldn't we go back to the castle and —"

"Yeah, we should. *After* lunch."

Aleta hesitated, then gave in. "Fine. Let's celebrate our break in the case with a break in our fast."

"*Now* you're gettin' the hang'a this. Let's go back t'the Seagull. I wanna see if Mannit's still there."

"To thank him?"

"That, too." Dru grinned. "Mostly I wanna hear about the Troll Riots."

Aleta chuckled, and Dru was pleased to hear himself chuckle back. He still missed Hawk, and still hated that more people gave a shit about the nobility than his partner. But Aleta was working out nicely, and life *did* go on. He'd done too many homicides to think any different.

"Also, you're buyin'," Dru added. "That's what rookies do on their first day, buy lunch for their partners."

"Really?" Aleta sounded dubious.

"Absolutely. It's a long-standing Guard tradition that I just made up a minute ago."

Aleta threw up her hands. "Oh, well, in that case, who am I to stand in the way?"

Dru laughed. It was the first time he'd truly laughed since Hawk died.

FIVE

Torin asked the question as he entered the alleyway between the Dog and Duck and Pyrin's Dry Goods in Dragon Precinct. Three guards from Dragon were already in the alleyway, one standing over a very short body, the other two holding the crowd of onlookers at bay — though there were fewer of the latter than usual, Torin noted. The guard with the body was Jared, to whom he had directed the query.

Next to him, Manfred chuckled. "That's usually the question you ask me."

"Used to be," Torin corrected gently.

Jared chuckled. "Lookit you, Manfred, all pretty in your brown cloak. Looks good on ya."

"Thanks, Jared."

Then Jared stared down at Manfred's belt. "What happened t'your sword?"

Torin smiled. Manfred was currently carrying one of the surplus swords from the castle's armory.

In reply, Manfred said, "I dropped my blade off with Molano to have it sharpened."

That earned him a snort from Jared. "Whatcher all fancy now, gotta get the elf lady t'make yer blade nice an' pretty?" Molano was an elven swordmaster, one of the finest in Cliff's End.

Manfred chuckled. "Something like that. So what *have* we got?"

"Victim's named Beffel. He's a halfling who was havin' a drink at the Dog an' Duck."

"A guest?" Manfred asked. Torin nodded his approval at his asking the right question.

Shaking his head, Jared said, "Nah, he just likes eatin' there. Lives in the Swamp, accordin' t'Olaf."

Olaf was the proprietor of the Dog and Duck. Torin noted that, while Beffel was unmoving, he was breathing. He asked, "Have you contacted the M.E.?"

"And a healer?" Manfred added. "He's still breathing."

Jared chuckled. "Yes t'both of you."

Manfred looked back at the crowd that the other two guards were holding back. "Any witnesses?"

"Nah, nobody saw nothin'. Couple people heard a fight, but by th'time they got out here, Beffel was down onna ground and the folks that beat 'im up were gone."

Regarding Torin quizzically, Manfred asked, "Should we talk to those couple of people?"

"Let's take a look at the victim first, shall we?" Torin approached Beffel as he spoke, Manfred following behind.

"Gotcherself some easy sailin' for this one," Jared said. "Boneen'll come by an' do the peel-back and you'll have your guys."

Boneen came to crime scenes and cast an Inanimate Residue, or "peel-back," spell which would reveal what happened in a given location in the recent past. Torin smiled. "It's not quite that simple, Jared. Boneen can tell us how many there were and what they look like, and what weapons they might have used, but he can't tell us where they are now."

Jared shrugged. "Fair 'nough."

Manfred knelt down by Beffel, the halfling's breaths steady, if shallow. Torin hoped the healer would arrive soon.

After a moment, Manfred pointed at the indentations on the halfling's right cheek. "Those look like knuckle marks." He lifted Beffel's tunic to expose his stomach, revealing more indentations of the same shape. "I'm thinking he was punched a lot. So Boneen probably won't see any weapons," he added with a smile.

Torin nodded in agreement.

"'Ey, Lieutenants!"

Turning, Torin saw one of the guards holding the crowd back standing next to a Temisan priest.

"We got us a healer!"

"Let him through." Torin was grateful that the healer arrived first. With luck, he'd be done by the time Boneen arrived. The peel-back only worked if there were no living creatures in the vicinity, excepting the spellcaster.

The priest was tall, overweight, and wearing the traditional red robes of a Temisan priest. His head was completely bald, save for a small tuft of hair on the crown tied into a top-knot, and he had a braided chin-beard. Both were blond flecked with gray. "I'm Brother Gambari."

"Lieutenant Torin ban Wyvald. Anything you could do for this poor halfling would be appreciated."

"Of course. What is his name?"

"Beffel."

Manfred was staring at Gambari, then looked at Jared. "You got a priest?"

Holding both hands palms-up, Jared said, "What? There's a Temisan church right over on Axe Lane."

"Yeah, and there's that healer right over on Boulder Pass."

Jared's face scrunched up. "What, that ugly half-dwarf crone?"

"She's not ugly!"

"Jared," Torin said quickly, "can you fetch the ones who found him?"

"Yeah, sure." He shot Manfred a look, then went off to do so.

The priest, for his part, was kneeling next to Beffel and placing his hands on the halfling's chest. After Gambari muttered a chant—the only words Torin could make out were "Beffel" and "Temisa"—a glow enveloped those hands, which spread to the halfling's chest a moment later.

As soon as Gambari removed his hands and stood up, Beffel's eyes lazily opened. "What—what happened?"

Holding out a hand for him, Torin said, "You were attacked, good sir. I'm Lieutenant ban Wyvald of the Castle Guard, this is my partner, Lieutenant Manfred."

Manfred, Torin noticed, beamed a bit at that.

"I—I—I don't—" Beffel shook his head, then finally took the proffered hand. Torin tugged gently to aid him to his feet. "Thank you, Lieutenant. I—I'm afraid I'm a bit scattered."

Gambari nodded. "He'll need a few moments to collect himself. I was able to heal all the damage, Mr. Beffel, but you will need to rest some."

Beffel frowned. "How do you know my name, priest?"

Defensively, Gambari said, "He told me," while pointing a long finger at Torin.

"And how'd *you* know it, Lieutenant?"

"I shared your name with the Castle Guard, Beffel," came a familiar voice from behind Torin.

Turning, Torin saw the diminutive form of Ubàrlig, the famous dwarven adventurer who had travelled with Gan Brightblade. Torin had first met the former general when he and Danthres investigated the murder of Brightblade and three of his and Ubàrlig's other comrades before midsummer.

Ubàrlig looked up at Torin. "Lieutenant ban Wyvald. It's a pleasure."

Torin couldn't entirely say the same, since the dwarf and his friends had done all they could to impede his and Danthres's investigation. The survivors then stuck around past midsummer creating more trouble. "I was not aware that you had returned to Cliff's End, General."

"I had accompanied Brother Genero back to Velessa, but after word of Lord Albin's death, I returned for the funeral."

"Just you?"

Ubàrlig smiled ruefully. "Worry not, Lieutenant, I'm alone. Bogg returned north, and Genero is still under investigation by the bishopric."

Gambari inserted himself into the conversation. "I'm sure the bishopric will exonerate Brother Genero. He is a great man, and I pray for him daily."

"Thank you." Ubàrlig nodded to the priest, then turned his attention back to Torin. "I have no intention of causing any trouble for you or Lieutenant Tresyllione. Where is your partner, anyhow?"

"She is my partner no longer. This is Lieutenant Manfred."

Manfred gave a slight bow. "It's an honor, sir."

"Well, you're certainly a more polite liar than Lieutenant Tresyllione. The honor is mine, Lieutenant Manfred."

"Excuse me, but may I go now?" Beffel asked the question, and Torin had to admit to having momentarily forgotten the halfling.

"I'm afraid not, Mr. Beffel. We need to know who attacked you."

"I—I'm afraid I didn't really—I mean . . ." Beffel blew out a breath. "Look, I just want to forget this happened."

Manfred stepped forward. "It's not that simple, Mr. Beffel. If these people attacked you, they could attack someone else. We need to know what happened."

"Worry not, young man," came a voice from the mouth of the alley, "we'll know as soon as you people get out of this alleyway."

Torin smiled as the M.E. waddled past the two guards. "Of course, Boneen. Come, Mr. Beffel, Brother Gambari, General Ubàrlig—let us leave the wizard to his magicks, and we'll continue this conversation in the street."

As they married action to Torin's words, the halfling glowered at Ubàrlig. "Why did you tell them my name?"

The dwarf stared at Beffel. "The first guard who came to investigate asked me. I was unaware that it was classified information."

"Look," Beffel said testily, "if I wanted to tell the Castle Guard my name, I'd tell them, and I'll thank you to mind your own business."

Manfred cut Ubàrlig off before he could reply. "Mr. Beffel, we have to question you about this. The lord and lady's law explicitly states that—"

"I thought Lord Albin died." Beffel folded his arms defiantly over his small chest.

"Yes," Manfred said slowly, "but his laws still—"

A blood-curdling scream came from the alley, and Torin found himself running to see what had happened before he even consciously acknowledged that he heard it. Manfred, Jared, the other two guards, and Ubàrlig were all right there with him.

Boneen was kneeling, the herbs and other spell components scattered around him on the ground, and his pestle was broken in three pieces. The wizard was drenched in sweat and breathing heavily.

Torin moved to help him to his feet. "What happened, Boneen?"

Between deep breaths, Boneen said, "A Keefda stone. Whoever assaulted that halfling had a blessed Keefda stone. It very—very *aggressively* blocks the use of magick in the vicinity of its activation for several days."

Torin had never heard of such a thing, but Ubàrlig apparently had. The dwarf stepped forward. "Keefda only made twelve of those—they were meant to be weapons against Chalmraik the Foul. But three of them were destroyed."

"Actually, six of them were." Boneen was now standing upright, and Torin let go of his arm. "Thank you, ban Wyvald. There are still a half-dozen of the stones at large."

Torin frowned. "I assume that the acquisition of such a stone would be prohibitively expensive?"

"The least I've heard of one selling for is five thousand gold pieces."

"What!?" Manfred made a choking noise as he cried out. Torin couldn't blame him. One thousand gold was an amount of coin the average person never even saw, much less five times that.

"It is a very rare and valuable item."

"So not something one would expect to see in the hands of barroom brawlers?" Torin asked the wizard.

"Hardly."

Torin turned back to look at the mouth of the alley — only to see no sign of the halfling in the crowd. "Where's Beffel?"

"Shit," one of the guards muttered, and he, his companion, and Jared all dashed back out onto the street.

Moments later, they came back. "He's gone."

Manfred turned to Torin. "Now what do we do?"

Ubàrlig said, "I'm more than happy to provide you with a description of the events."

Torin winced. The notion of the general attempting to be helpful was one that filled him with dread. "Did you actually witness the assault?"

"No, but I can describe what it sounded like."

With a sigh, Torin said, "Very well, come back to the castle with us and we'll take a statement. Perhaps we shall be lucky. Jared, tell Sergeant Grint to put out an all-points on Beffel."

"You bet. Don't worry, Lieutenant, we'll find the little shit."

Manfred smirked at Torin. "I know that look on Jared's face, Lieutenant. He hates being made a fool of. He won't rest until Beffel's found."

"Good to know. Because without him, there really isn't much of a case." Torin smiled. "And we're equals now, Manfred. You may call me 'Torin.' Indeed, you could have before as well."

"Sorry, Lieu — er, Torin. Habit, you know?"

"Of course." He glanced at Ubàrlig. "Come, General, let us go to the castle and see what we might salvage from this."

"I'll join you, ban Wyvald." Boneen still sounded a bit ragged. "I'm afraid I don't have the capacity for a Teleport Spell just at the moment."

Torin's eyes went wide. Boneen's preferred exit from a crime scene was always to teleport. The fact that the effects of this Keefda stone were that extensive indicated all the more that this was more than just a simple assault.

SIX

Danthres ground her teeth in annoyance as she somehow managed not to point out that this was the fifth time that Sir Lio had said that what happened was terrible. She and Kellan were sitting in his office, barely able to even see the transport minister over the schedules for ships and caravans and reports from various guilds that were piled on his desk.

The nobleman went on. "I feel like I've been hit in the knees repeatedly. Just an awful blow to the city-state."

"What we need to know, Sir Lio, is if you can think of anyone who might have had reason to kill Lord Albin."

"Kill? I thought he died from his illness. He got that every year at this time, you know. Just awful. I always said it would kill him some day, and here I see I was right. It's so terrible, what happened, isn't it?"

Speaking slowly mostly to avoid yelling, Danthres said, "We need to investigate the possibility that he was murdered, Sir Lio. Rule it out, at the very least."

"Rule what out? Don't be ridiculous, everyone loved Lord Albin. Honestly, I think he was more loved than the king and queen." He chuckled. "Unless you suppose the king and queen killed him out of jealousy?"

Frowning, Kellan said, "You think that's a possibility?"

Danthres rolled her eyes, even as Sir Lio said, "No, of course not! Goodness, what kind of imbeciles are they employing as guards these days? My point is that no one wished him ill. Except for some peasants, perhaps, but how would they have killed him? Anyhow, it doesn't matter, it was the illness that killed him. It's so terrible, isn't it?"

Realizing that they were getting nowhere—again—Danthres got up from the guest chair. "Thank you for your time, Sir Lio. If you think of anything, please send a messenger to the east wing."

"There's nothing to think of." Sir Lio shook his head and went back to his schedules. "There's no one who wanted Lord Albin dead."

"HALF THE CASTLE WANTED LORD ALBIN DEAD."

Madam Brigit hadn't been in her office when Danthres and Kellan came by, but her secretary—a harried, halfling woman—said she was in the dining hall preparing for Lord Blayk's first state dinner, and she was *very* busy and probably wouldn't have much time to talk, but if they wished they could try to speak to her while she worked as she was *very* busy and wouldn't have time for them at all otherwise.

As they had approached the dining room, Kellan had asked, "How busy can the person who plans the banquets *be*?"

"I thought the same thing until I met Madam Brigit the first time nine years ago." Danthres had shaken her head with amusement at the memory. "It's rather like battle strategy, making sure every arrangement is precisely perfect without offending any of the dozens of participants, all of whom are easily offended at the most idiotic things."

Right now, Brigit was supervising the placement of the name cards on the table, which was being done by two pagegirls. "No, no, girl, Sir Palrik can't sit next to the Fansarris. They hate each other. And don't put him next to Sir Rommett, he's left handed and they'll clash elbows. Also Sir Palrik tends to gnaw on his meat, so don't have him face Madam Ylrik, as she does not consume meat and tends to lecture on the subject of those who do."

The girl frowned. "Won't anybody sittin' 'cross from 'er be eatin' meat?"

"Yes, girl," Brigit said, exasperatedly, "but Sir Palrik is particularly vulgar in his consumption of it, and is highly likely to set Madam Ylrik off. Put one of the daintier eaters across from her. Sir Rommett, perhaps—no, wait, he must sit near to the lord and lady, and Lady Meerka finds Madam Ylrik tiresome." She shook her head, then turned back to Danthres. "Where was I?"

"You said that half the castle—" Danthres started.

"Yes, they all hated Lord Albin, may Mitre grant him safe passage to the afterlife, even though they pretended they loved him. No, girl, I told you, Sir Palrik is left-handed, so his forks must go on the right."

"So was there anyone in particular who wanted him dead?" Danthres asked.

Brigit shook her head. "It'd take less time if I listed who didn't. Sir Rommett loved him all to pieces, but Lord Albin made him chamberlain after Sir Gevlin passed on, may Mitre grant him safe passage to the afterlife."

"How did *you* feel about him?"

"Well, I would've liked it if he held fewer banquets, or at least invited fewer people to 'em, and most of his demands were hilarious, but that merely made him annoying, not worthy of a journey to the afterlife."

Guided by Mitre, no doubt, Danthres managed to stop herself from saying. "Did anyone recently have a particular grudge against him?"

"Well, Sir and Madam Fansarri were upset because Lord Albin didn't stop the Brotherhood of Wizards from censuring their boy when he studied magick on his own. As if he *could've* done anything. But I doubt either of them did it, they're all talk, those two. No, girl, don't put Sir Louff there, he's very old and can't hear out of his left ear. He needs to be on the end." She turned back to Danthres. "Look, I'm sorry, I have to get this done. Lord Blayk could've at least waited another week so folks could mourn before holding the dinner. You want a suspect, talk to the whole blessed castle, that's what I say."

As they left the dining room, Kellan shook his head. "How is it that she can keep track of who eats what, who's left-handed, who's deaf in one hear, who hates who, but she can't remember the pagegirls' names?"

Danthres snorted. "You heard the pagegirls talk. They're not upper-class—probably the daughters of someone's secretary. Nobility rarely bother to remember the names of anyone who doesn't have a prefix."

Kellan smiled. "That include 'Lieutenant'?"

Unable to help smiling back—which was twice in one day while in the presence of her unwanted new partner—Danthres said, *"Especially* 'Lieutenant'."

"WHAT, POISONED? NO, NOT POSSIBLE. BUT THEN, IT MIGHT BE POSSIBLE. I suppose. Who do you think did it?"

Danthres was mildly amused that her and Kellan's next stop was Sir Palrik, given what they'd just learned about his eating habits from Madam Brigit. He was smoking a pipe while sitting at his desk, which, in contrast to that of Sir Lio, was empty. As the chief military advisor to the lord and lady, his job was fairly unnecessary, since the Castle Guard was under the purview of Sir Rommett, Cliff's End had no standing army as such, and King Marcus and Queen Marta weren't at war with anybody.

In answer to his question, Danthres said, "We're not sure, Sir Palrik, that's why we're talking to you and the other people in the castle."

"Ah, yes, I see. Weren't you partnered with ban Wyvald? I served with him under your Captain Osric back during the elven wars. Nasty business, that. Did ban Wyvald go and retire along with Osric?"

"No, he simply has a new partner. I was wondering—"

"Those were some heady times, though, I can tell you. Oh, it was mostly awful, but Osric was a damn fine commander. You're lucky to have had him for so long. But I suppose he earned his retirement."

Danthres refrained from comment, given that Osric was basically forced out and replaced with an imbecile. "Sir Palrik, we'd like to know who you think might want to have poisoned Lord Albin."

"Poisoned? Oh, that's unlikely. Isn't it? Look, I'm more than happy to think about it, if you like, but I don't see how it's even possible." He took a thoughtful puff on his pipe. "Well, there was that one fella."

Finally! Danthres was barely able to contain herself enough not to say that out loud. "Who might that be?"

"There was this pageboy who was fired for spilling wine. He swore that he'd kill Lord Albin for getting him fired. Annoying little lad, name of Del Francit."

Again, Danthres had to restrain herself, this time from cheering, since they finally had a lead.

But then she noticed Kellan wincing. Glaring at him, she said, "What is it, Kellan?"

"I, ah, know Del Francit."

"Good."

"No, ma'am, er, bad. Del Francit died in a brawl at the Ogre's Breath two weeks ago. I remember the bartender tellin' me that Francit used t'work at the castle 'til he got fired."

Palrik nodded. "Yes, yes, that's definitely him."

Danthres sighed. "We'll look into him anyhow, in case he had friends."

"That's an excellent idea, Lieutenant!" Palrik pointed at her with the end of his pipe before putting it back in his mouth. "And if I think of anything else, I'll be sure to inform you. Unless I don't, in which case I won't."

Shaking her head, Danthres got up, Kellan following behind.

"IT'S THE GUILDS. THEY'RE ALL OUT TO GET US."

Sir and Madam Wint jointly ran the ministry of construction. Any time something was built or torn down in Cliff's End, these two had to approve it.

"The day Lord Albin died," Madam Wint was saying, "Sir Rommett was to meet with the guilds to discuss the new tariffs."

"They weren't happy," Sir Wint added. "Not even a little bit."

"They were threatening work stoppages, can you believe that?"

"I—" Danthres started, but Madam Wint kept going.

"Of all the cheek!"

"Indeed," Sir Wint said. "They just don't understand the financial realities, they're simply being filthy greedheads."

"If there's anything I can't stand," Madam Wint added, "it's filthy greedheads."

"And they're all trying to get organized!" Sir Wint cried before Danthres could again attempt to ask a question. "It'll be the doom of us all."

"And I'm sure they were behind Lord Albin's death."

"Absolutely sure, it couldn't possibly have been anyone else."

There was a brief silence, and Danthres almost fell over from the shock of them stopping talking long enough for her to speak. "How do you think they did it?"

Sir Wint was aghast. "How should *we* know?"

"We're civilized people," Madam Wint added. "We don't know how thugs work."

"But they must have done it. Who else could it possibly be?"

"THE GUILDS? NO, THAT'S ABSURD."

Danthres had deliberately chosen Sir Rommett as the last interview because she had assumed it would be the most unpleasant, given her tumultuous history with the bureaucrat in question. She and Rommett had clashed any number of times in the past. Danthres had considered resigning more than once just so she would never have to deal with him again.

However, she reckoned without considering the capacity for the other nobles in the castle to piss her off. Her mood, which was foul before she began, was bordering on murderous.

"We have evidence that the guilds might have been responsible," Danthres said. "In fact, we were told that you were to meet with them the day you found Lord Albin's body."

"Yes, about the new tariffs. But I did meet with them, the day before the funeral—for obvious reasons, the meeting that day was put off—and they agreed to accept the new tariffs out of respect for Lord Albin's passing. Not only that, but all the arrangements at Jayka Park were donated by the various guilds, free of charge, out of respect."

Danthres sighed. She should have realized that this was too good to be true. "Might at least one of the guilds decided they didn't wish to put up with the tariffs and taken action?"

Rommett shook his head. "I suppose it's possible, of course, but—" He let out a breath. "Look, I'm not a fool, I'm aware that some of the guilds do use intimidation tactics to achieve their ends. But I doubt this was one of them, if for no other reason than it was such an abject failure. It *didn't* achieve the end of lowering the tariffs, and *every* guild leader was in agreement that they would accept them without complaint. And it's rare that they all agree on the fact that the sky is blue."

Rising to her feet, Danthres said, "So you don't think anyone killed him, either. Wonderful."

"Actually . . ." Rommett trailed off.

Danthres sat back down. "What is it, Sir Rommett?"

"Well, I didn't really think about it much at the time, as I was in shock, but—Lord Albin was going to meet with me that morning about a matter of grave importance."

"Can you be more specific?"

"I wish I could," Rommett said emphatically. For the first time in the conversation — or, indeed, ever — Danthres observed the chamberlain's emotional state. He was noticeably distraught. "He didn't tell me! He just said it was a 'grave matter' and that he'd explain at the meeting. It may be nothing, but I just don't know." He looked up and stared right at Danthres. "I'm glad you're investigating this, Lieutenant. I've been worried about this for a while now, and the truth needs to come out."

As Danthres came into the squadroom, Kellan trailing uselessly behind her as he had been all day, she heard Torin's voice coming from Osric's — or, rather, Grovis's office.

I'm never going to get used to that.

"I've got the guards at Dragon looking for Beffel, but in the meantime —"

"In the *meantime*, Torin," Grovis said archly, "I don't see the point of pursuing this. General Ubàrlig's statement isn't of particular use, as he didn't actually *see* anything. The only true witness is the victim, who's disappeared. I don't see why you wish to continue to investigate so minor an incident. Nor indeed why you should."

Danthres put her head in her hands. She hadn't known that Ubàrlig was back in Cliff's End, and she wondered if the other two idiots were with him.

"Because the magick used to block the peel-back is rare and expensive, far too much so to be used to hide the evidence of a simple assault outside a tavern. It's akin to using a Fireball Spell to kill a single insect. That makes it less than minor."

"In *your* opinion. In mine, this is a waste of your valuable time."

"Grovis, I need to pursue this, if for no other reason than the Brotherhood will —"

Now Grovis got all prim. "I'll thank you, *Lieutenant*, to refer to me by my rank. And I'll be the one to determine what you should or shouldn't 'need' to pursue. I tolerated your japes and jibes when we were equals, but I'm your superior and I expect to be treated as such. Unless the victim steps forward, there's nothing to pursue, and you will not pursue it, but put yourself and Manfred back in the rotation. Don't walk out on me!"

Torin had, in fact, walked out on him, stalking straight past Danthres and Kellan and leaving the squadroom, just as Manfred came in. "Lieu— er, Torin, I escorted Ubàrlig out, what do you—" But Torin was already past Manfred by that point, having stormed out without speaking to anyone.

Wryly, Danthres said, "That's usually *my* behavior."

"Is he always like that?" Manfred asked.

"No." Danthres grew serious. "And that's cause for concern. I'll talk to him when he gets back."

"Thanks." Manfred smiled. "I'm glad you're talking to me, Danthres."

She scowled at him. "We're colleagues, why wouldn't I talk to you?" She knew the answer to that, of course, and also knew why he was pleasantly surprised that she was speaking to him now, but she really hoped he understood that it was *not* something she wished to discuss in the squadroom.

"Danthres, I need to talk to you." Grovis was now standing in the doorway to the office, arms folded over the gryphon crest on the chest of his armor. He still looked ridiculous in the purple cloak. But then, he always looked ridiculous, regardless of what he might be wearing.

Wincing, Danthres said, "And there's one answer to that question."

"He's not a colleague, he's a superior," Manfred said.

"In fact, he's neither, and that he outranks us is the only reason why I'm willing to talk to *him*." She turned around. "What is it, Grovis?"

Grovis attempted to glower at Danthres, though his fishlike face wasn't suited to the expression. "As I told your erstwhile partner, I'll thank you to refer to me by rank."

"You'll only thank me if I do it, Grovis. What do you want?"

"An update, if you please. I understand that Lady Meerka herself requested you conduct this investigation, so I wish to be updated."

Danthres sighed. "I wish I had something to update you with."

"You spent all day talking to the nobility! Why don't you have anything?"

"Because we spent all day talking to the nobility. They don't seem to know anything." She glanced at Kellan. "And I had to do all the questioning."

Kellan sighed. "I'm sorry, Danthres, but I'm just—" He sighed again. "I grew up in Goblin. This whole world of fancy nobles and nice clothes is just—intimidating."

Manfred put a hand on his friend's shoulder. "They're *people*, Arn, just like anyone else, except richer."

"Hardly that," Grovis said. "They are the best of us."

"Not when it comes to paying attention to their surroundings, they aren't." Danthres snarled. "Half of them don't believe Albin was killed, the other half believe in absurd conspiracy theories. The only thing that was useful came from Sir Rommett, of all people, but that just opens more questions." She briefly filled Grovis in on Rommett's aborted and mysterious meeting with Albin.

Grovis rubbed his chin. "You should talk to Lord Albin's secretary."

"Unfortunately, Lord Blayk let her go, and we were told that she boarded a boat to Saptor Isle this morning."

"Oh dear."

Danthres had used stronger language when she was told. "I'd like to have Torin back on this. You seem to want to take him off his current case in any event, and Kellan and I aren't meshing."

"Hey, that ain't fair, Danthres!" Kellan said. "It's just—"

Grovis held up a hand. "It doesn't matter. Lord Blayk himself assigned you to Kellan, and I won't gainsay his rightful authority without a better reason than your desires." He turned to go back into Osric's old office—Danthres refused to think of it as his—and then called back over his shoulder. "Besides, that would be doing you a favor, and since you seem to believe that I am not worthy of respect, I have no motivation to do that favor, now do I?"

Danthres let out a breath through her teeth. She supposed she deserved that. "At least Grovis is getting the hang of the political aspects of the job."

"Is that a good thing?" Kellan asked.

"For him, certainly. For us, probably not. Osric used his political skills to shield us from the shit streaming forth from the wing of the castle that we just left. I doubt Grovis will be so considerate."

"Excuse me, Lieutenant Tresyllione?"

Turning, Danthres saw one of the guards assigned to the castle, whose name she couldn't bring herself to care enough to remember, standing in the doorway, his considerable bulk blocking the person standing behind him. "Yes?"

"Gentleman here to see you, ma'am."

He stepped aside to reveal the face of a fellow halfbreed she hadn't seen in almost twenty years. Unlike Danthres, his face combined the prettier aspects of both human and elven features.

Danthres scowled at him. "I was warned you'd be showing up. What did you do to Sorlin, Javian?"

Shaking his head, Javian chuckled. "I see the years haven't changed you a bit, Thressa. It's good to see you, too."

"Who's this?" Manfred asked, sounding confused.

"This is Elsthar Javian, the former head of the ruling council in Sorlin—and the one who kicked me out of there."

SEVEN

TORIN STOMPED THROUGH THE SQUADROOM, STOMPED THROUGH THE CASTLE corridors, stomped out through the portcullis, and stomped down Meerka Way before he even realized what he was doing.

He couldn't recall the last time he was this angry or out of sorts. Well, no, that wasn't true, he could remember being out of sorts not that long ago when his father came to visit.

But even the unexpected arrival of Wyvald ban Garin in Cliff's End didn't quite anger Torin as much as Grovis's dismissal of the Beffel case. It frustrated him because Osric would have trusted his judgment and let him pursue it. Even back during the war, Osric had always listened to Torin.

Being fobbed off like that, especially by Grovis — who was barely competent as a detective, much less a captain — angered Torin to a degree he wouldn't have credited himself capable of.

Yet here he was, so furious he walked out of the castle in the middle of his shift.

He strode past Oak Way and the many new mansions that had been built upon it of late, crossing into Dragon Precinct. At that point, the thoroughfare became a bit more crowded, with people giving Torin a wide berth.

Torin didn't stop until he reached Boulder Pass. Turning left, he found himself soon standing in front of the building where Osric rented a flat.

Half a dozen large burly men, and one burly woman, were carrying furniture out the front door and loading it onto a horse-drawn cart. Another woman stood by the two horses that were tethered to the cart's front end, petting them and occasionally feeding them apples. Horses were rarely seen within the Cliff's End city limits outside of Unicorn

Precinct—several stables located on the outskirts of the demesne did excellent business taking care of horses whose owners had business in town—but when one did see them, they were usually serving a cargo-carrying function of some sort, as these were. The thoroughfares of Dragon, Goblin, and Mermaid were just too crowded to accommodate a horse that was moving at anything faster than a very slow trot.

Osric himself was directing one of the burly men, who was carrying a table. Upon catching sight of Torin, he broke off from his discussion and approached him with a sardonic smile. Torin noted that Osric hadn't shaved since the day of the funeral, and his trademark stubble was already starting to come back into place. "Aren't you on shift, ban Wyvald?"

Torin grinned broadly. "I had a bit of a disagreement with your replacement and needed to blow off some steam."

"Thought you had Tresyllione for that."

"Ah, well, Lord Blayk—in addition to forcing you to retire—also separated me and Danthres."

"So he's an even bigger damn fool than I thought."

Glancing over at the movers, Torin asked, "I take it you're no longer satisfied with your accommodations?"

Osric laughed at that, which surprised Torin. He couldn't recall the last time he heard the man laugh. "Something like that, yes, ban Wyvald. You see, I took that flat when I first was offered the job of captain of the Castle Guard by Lord Albin eleven years ago. It was cheap and tiny, but I didn't anticipate that the job would last a year. I expected the Castle Guard to fail in its mandate, or at the very least for me to fail in the running of it. So I kept a small, cheap apartment with minimal furnishings. That grew into a habit, one I never changed after more than a decade. Besides, after the disaster with our pensions following the war, I became somewhat frugal. I wished to have savings of my own for a change."

Torin nodded. A percentage of their wages earned by serving as soldiers in the king and queen's service against the Elf Queen had supposedly been set aside for their pensions. They were both surprised to learn after that war that said percentage had instead been funneled right back into the war effort, leaving any soldiers who survived the war to be out of luck with regard to their promised post-service compensation.

"Now, though, I've saved quite a bit of gold, and it's time I put it to good use. I've purchased a house on Alfar's Way."

"Excellent! That's fine news, Captain."

Osric put a hand on Torin's shoulder and smiled. "You don't need to call me that, anymore, ban Wyvald. It's Osric. You adjusted from 'General' to 'Captain' easy enough a decade ago, seems to me you can do the same with this."

"And yet you were never able to call me 'Torin' no matter how many times I asked."

That got Osric to laugh again. "Very true. Years of habit, I suppose. But I shall endeavor to do so."

"Oh, I'm used to it now. It was more of an issue when we first served together. At the time, I didn't appreciate being reminded of the fact that I was the son of Wyvald ban Garin."

"So what brings you to see me?"

Torin let out a very long breath. "I just—I feel as if I've lost so much in so short an amount of time. I barely had time to realize that Hawk was dead when we learned that Lord Albin was dead as well. Then I lost my captain and my partner on top of that."

"So you're feeling a bit lost?"

"I wasn't actually, at first. But when Grovis tried to take me off the Beffel case . . ." Torin shook his head. "I haven't been this angry, this confused, this out of sorts, since I first signed up to fight against the Elf Queen." He gave Osric a small smile. "You helped me through that then, and I suppose I'm hoping you'll do the same now."

"What exactly is the problem with Grovis?"

Torin explained the particulars of the Beffel case, interrupted a few times by Osric having to answer a question posed by his movers.

"Grovis doesn't understand the importance of the Keefda stone. It affected Boneen so much that he didn't even have the wherewithal to cast a Teleport Spell." Torin sighed. "Part of my frustration is that you've always trusted my judgment in these matters. If I, or Danthres, had come to you with this, you would have allowed me to pursue this case."

Osric chuckled and shook his head. "What a short memory you have, ban Wyvald."

Frowning, Torin said, "Excuse me?"

"I was with you until you used the word 'always.' True, I've *mostly* trusted your judgment, but that trust took some time to develop. Remember the Smapp case?"

Torin nodded. That was his and Danthres's third case together. "I kept insisting that Sir Sheeler be brought in for questioning. You and Danthres both disagreed with me."

"Because you had no kind of evidence, certainly not enough to bring in someone as prominent as Sir Sheeler. In fact, I thought you were mad to consider him."

"But I was right." Torin remembered the case well, as it was both Sir and Madam Sheeler who had killed Lin Smapp as part of a bizarre sexual ritual.

"Eventually, yes, you were able to prove it, but it wasn't until a few days later when you gathered sufficient evidence that I was willing to let you question a noble on the subject. And then there was the brawl in the Dancing Seagull, where you went against the peel-back."

Torin frowned. "I didn't, I simply said that the person dressed as a sailor wasn't an actual sailor. I was right about that one, too, he was wearing his brother's raiments."

"And then there was the Kayt case."

Shaking his head ruefully, Torin said, "I admit, I was wrong about that one."

"You see my point, though? Trust was something you had to earn with me. And, I might add, that in all three of those cases, you continued to follow your instincts despite what I told you, and in the end you and Tresyllione closed all three."

"A fair point, but—" Torin threw up his hands in frustration. "In none of those cases did you take me off it—though, as I recall, you threatened to do so in the Smapp case."

Osric shrugged. "Sir Gevlin was pressuring me to leave the Sheelers out of the investigation, despite the fact that the victim was obviously known to them."

"Of course." Torin nodded and stared down at the ground for a moment. "We need you back, Osric. You always served as a wall between us and the imbeciles in the nobility. Grovis *is* one of the imbeciles in the nobility. Danthres may not last a full month."

But Osric was shaking his head. "You don't need me, ban Wyvald. When I first took the job, when I first promoted Tresyllione, when I first brought you in, yes, I would agree with you. Back then, the Castle

Guard's mandate as an investigatory agency was relatively new. And my predecessor had made a troll's ear out of it. But now? The Guard is bigger than me, bigger than Grovis—bigger even than Albin's son. You heard the king before the funeral—he's trying to replicate this in the other large city-states. At this point, even Grovis can't ruin it."

"Perhaps not, but he's like to try. Especially if he keeps insisting on taking me off cases."

"Let me ask you something, ban Wyvald—did Grovis formally order you to stop investigating?"

Torin thought back to Grovis's diatribe. "He said that until the victim was found, for Manfred and I to go back into the rotation."

Osric's eye widened. "So they did promote Manfred. Good. I always liked him. Did they promote Kellan, too?"

Nodding, Torin said, "And Aleta."

For the first time since his arrival, Torin saw the trademark Osric scowl, which he had to admit to missing. Osric's deep scowl was a major component of any conversation with him, and its absence until now was peculiar to say the least. "Why three? Manfred and Kellan replaced Hawk and Grovis, but—"

"Iaian also retired."

"Hah!" The scowl was replaced by a wide-mouthed, nasty laugh. "That mad old hobgoblin actually took a lesser pension? And I don't get to enjoy it?"

"Not entirely. Lord Blayk offered him the full twenty-five if he retired now, same as he offered you."

"Wish I'd thought of that." Osric shook his head. "In any case, I've never known you or Tresyllione to be swayed by the opinions of people you don't respect. And over the past several years, I've seen nothing to indicate that you respect Grovis's."

Torin smiled. "True."

While most of the burly men were loading a chair onto the cart, the burly woman walked over to the pair of them. "'Scuse me, Mr. Osric, sir, but we're all done-like."

"Good, Aeris, thank you. Aeris, this is a former employee of mine, Lieutenant Torin ban Wyvald."

"Pleasure, sir." Aeris gave Torin a brief two-fingered salute.

"Aeris here runs the Faltang Moving Company."

Torin frowned. "I know that name."

"Dru and Hawk arrested Mel Faltang for fraud two years ago."

Aeris let out a gap-toothed grin. "I was workin' for 'im at th'time."

Osric added, "She was also the main witness."

"I went an' bought the comp'ny so's Faltang could be payin' 'is debts off. Last I heard, he was movin' t'Barlin." She regarded Torin quizzically. "I don't suppose you'll need anyone t'be movin' nothin', will you, Lieutenant ban Wyvald, sir?"

"Not at present, no." Torin smiled. "But assuming you get everything to Osric's new home in one piece, I will be sure to get in touch should the need arise."

"Very kind of you, sir, thankee." She went over to the cart. "All right, girls 'n' boys, let's get movin'!"

Osric called out, "I'll meet you at the house!"

The woman with the horses grabbed the reins and tugged on them. The horses started to slowly amble forward even as three of the men moved to walk in front of the horses, clearing a path for them. Not that they were moving fast enough to endanger anyone, but it was good to keep the way clear as much as possible.

As they went off, Torin gave his former commander a grateful nod. "Thank you, Osric. I appreciate you talking me through this."

"My pleasure—" Osric smiled. "—Torin."

They both chuckled, and Torin said, "Good luck with the move."

Torin walked past the cart and headed back toward Meerka Way. It was time to get back to work.

EIGHT

At first, Danthres had absolutely no idea what she was supposed to do with Javian, besides possibly run him through with her sword. But doing that in the middle of the squadroom in front of Manfred, Kellan, and the guard would be problematic.

Aleta and Dru walked in shortly after Javian, thus providing more witnesses to her theoretical homicide. They had found the name of their suspect, which Danthres uncharitably assumed to be entirely due to Dru's efforts. They had a guard bring the newly identified Gobink up from the hole and then Dru showed Aleta how to interact with Ep, the imp who kept the Castle Guard's files, and then how to change the paperwork to add the suspect's name.

There was still a free interview room, so Danthres took Javian in there. This conversation needed to happen in private.

As soon as Danthres closed the door, Javian asked, "Isn't this where you question people you think commit a crime?"

"Yes." Danthres walked past Javian to stand near the table.

He regarded her quizzically. "Do you believe I've committed a crime?"

"Some of those we bring in here are people we only suspect of such, and the questions we ask are designed to learn if they are or not."

"Well, let's hope I depart the premises not in chains, then." Javian leaned against the wall near the lantern that was the room's only light source. It cast shadows on his elegant cheekbones. "Who told you I was coming to Cliff's End?"

Danthres frowned. "Hm?" Then she recalled what she'd said to Javian when he'd entered the squadroom. "An elf named Fanthral."

Javian rolled his eyes. "Oh for Wiate's sake, did that idiot bring his absurd quest for members of the Elf Queen's court to Cliff's End?"

Danthres sighed, annoyed at the memory of Fanthral sweeping through the castle demanding his way. "Yes."

"I don't suppose he found any?"

"One, but he was already dead."

Javian grinned his widest smile. Danthres had forgotten how wide-mouthed he was, resulting in a smile that almost seemed to double the width of his face. "Please tell me that he didn't find a necromancer to animate the elf's corpse so he could trundle it back to the Consortium?"

Unable to help herself, Danthres chuckled at the image. "No, but only because he didn't think of it. Besides, he got in enough hot water with the Brotherhood with the shitstorm he stirred up."

"Fitting, since he spent his entire time in Sorlin annoying people."

"He did the same here, believe me." Danthres shook her head. "Dammit!"

Frowning, Javian asked, "What is it, Thressa?"

"It's 'Danthres.' Nobody's called me 'Thressa' for twenty years."

"To be honest, I don't think I can possibly refer to you as anything else."

"What are you doing here?" Danthres asked angrily. "Why aren't you in Sorlin running the council?"

"There *is* no council, Thressa — sorry, *Danthres* — and I don't rule it. With the rise of the Consortium to rule the elven lands, the purity laws were officially revoked. But even before that, the community was already dying."

"'How's that possible? What did you do to drive people away? Or did you just kick them out like you did me?"

No longer was there a trace of a smile on Javian's face, which suited Danthres just fine. She wanted this to be an unpleasant conversation, not the happy reunion she feared it would become if she and Javian retreated into their usual banter.

He looked away from her. "You were only the third person in Sorlin's history to be asked to leave, Thressa. And also the last. Since the Elf Queen's fall, people started leaving of their own volition, wishing to return to their homes." He turned to look at her with an expression of sadness. It just made Danthres want to punch him. "After the official repealing of the purity laws last year, we had a mass exodus. By the time that idiot Fanthral showed up we were below subsistence levels. The council voted to disband the community, and it passed unanimously."

"As head of the council, you could've vetoed —"

"No, I couldn't have." Javian walked up to Danthres and put a hand on each shoulder, staring at her intently with those deep blue eyes that came from his elven mother. Indeed, Danthres could remember Shantha giving her the exact same stare when she was a little girl and had done something wrong when she and Javian and Lil were playing together.

Thinking of Lil just made Danthres angrier, and she shrugged off Javian's arms and turned away.

"Thressa," he said, "I'm not head of the council anymore."

"What?"

The wide smile came back. "Well, technically, *nobody* is, now."

"Javian . . ."

He grew serious again. "I haven't been head of the council for twenty years."

Danthres's eyes widened. "Since — ?"

"Yes." Javian nodded. "The last vote that I supervised was the one to expel you from Sorlin. I resigned from the council chair after that."

"Why? You were the best chair Sorlin ever had."

He stared at her. "You *know* why."

Danthres looked away, again unwilling to look into those blue eyes.

She stared instead at the far wall on the other side of the table. "So what happens next?"

"I was going to take a boat to Saptor Isle to retire. It's past time, to be honest. Even if Sorlin was still intact, I don't really have —"

Danthres whirled around to face him. "I don't mean what happens next to *you*. I don't give a damn what happens next to *you*," she lied, "since you don't seem to care about anything that matters anymore. But what happens next to the people like me, or like Sharr, or like Zeen, or like you? What happens when the Consortium inevitably collapses under the weight of its own idiocy, just like every other pathetic attempt at a government they've tried since the end of the war, and it gets replaced by something a lot more hidebound? What happens when the purity laws are reinstated?"

Javian shrugged. "*If* that happens, then someone will no doubt found another place very much like Sorlin. But it will have to have someone else to administer it." He shook his head. "Thressa, after Lil died, I just — I just couldn't go on. Being forced to expel you was the final line of the spell of discontentment that Lil's death cast upon me."

Danthres glowered at him. "For the record? There are many things about living in Sorlin that I've missed these past twenty years. Your pathetic metaphors are *not* one of them."

Javian laughed. "Whereas I have very much missed your bluntness."

She pointed an accusatory finger at him. "You're avoiding the subject, Tharri. What I went through, what we all went through, can't be allowed to happen again. Remember all the mass graves?"

Gently, Javian said, "That hasn't happened in years, Thressa." Then he smiled. "And it's good to hear you call me 'Tharri' again."

"What?" Danthres thought back on her conversation with Javian. "I didn't."

"You absolutely did." He laughed. "It's all right, it was good to hear."

She couldn't believe it. Two decades away from her childhood friend, twenty years of hating him and what he had done to her life, and in just a few minutes was back into old habits.

The only ones who called him "Tharri" were Danthres herself and Lil. Which meant nobody had called him that since Lil died. As far as Danthres was concerned, after that, he was Javian.

"Look, I'm staying at the Dog and Duck until I can find a boat to book passage on. You should join me for dinner tonight—or tomorrow night, if you can't do tonight."

Danthres's eyes widened. "How'd you get a room at the Dog and Duck?"

Javian's wide smile came back. "I didn't arrive in Cliff's End until the day of Lord Albin's funeral. A rather large number of rooms became available once the, ah, festivities had ended."

Shuddering, Danthres said, "Your timing was impeccable. It was worse than midsummer here for the week leading up to the funeral."

He turned toward the door, then looked back at Danthres. "I am free to go, yes, Thressa?"

For a brief, insane moment, Danthres considered arresting him. The fact that she couldn't even dredge up a fake charge was the only thing that stopped her, and even then she seriously thought about it. Finally, however, she just stared back at him. "Get out of here, Javian."

He opened the door and then stopped halfway through the threshold without looking back at her. "You know, Thressa, I've really missed you. It was hard enough losing Lil, but losing you right after that—it almost broke me."

Danthres snarled. "Then you shouldn't have kicked me out."

That did get Javian to turn back around. "I didn't kick you out, Thressa. And you know that. You caused the vote, and there was no other way for the vote to go once it was called. Not after what you did."

Pointing at the doorway he was standing in, Danthres said, "Will you go away, please, Javian?"

He took a bow toward her. "Best of luck to you—Lieutenant Tresyllione." Again, the wide-mouthed smile, and then he left.

Manfred, who was talking with Kellan, watched him leave and then got up and walked over to Danthres. "Are you all right?"

"Why wouldn't I be?"

Indicating with his head the doorway to the corridor through which Javian had just left, Manfred asked, "Is he an old lover of yours?"

Danthres barked a laugh. "I'd sooner have slept with my brother—if I had a brother." She sighed. "He was the closest I came to one."

Both Manfred and Kellan were looking at her expectantly, as if expecting her to go on.

But she'd said more than she'd intended to either of these two. Her sleeping with Manfred once didn't entitle him to know the details of her life, nor did Kellan being partnered with her for a single, unproductive day.

The time chimes rang out nineteen times. When they were done, Danthres let out a long breath. "I'm going home."

Without another word she left the squadroom.

NINE

GOBINK SIGHED AS HE WAS BROUGHT UP FROM THE BASEMENT DUNGEON TO the featureless, windowless room in the eastern wing of the castle for the third time. The room was actually worse than the cell. At least in the dungeons—the locals called it "the hole," due he supposed to it being underground—you had some notion of the passage of time. The cells themselves had no windows, but the end of the corridor did have one, and the sun cast shadows throughout the day, and occasionally you got glances of moonlight.

This room, though, just off the Cloaks' office space, had no connection to the outside unless the door was open, which it never was unless someone was entering or departing. The sole source of light was a single lantern.

Gobink hated being confined. It was why he spent so much time at sea.

He wondered if it would be a third set of Cloaks who talked to him this time. Maybe, he'd get the two humans—the half-elf bitch and the snotty elven woman were both really annoying, but they each had a human male partner who was at least tolerable.

Not that it mattered. He wasn't going to say a damn thing. Both his debts and his family were taken care of and it didn't matter if he died. If he hadn't taken on this job, he'd be dead already.

The gambling had gotten out of control, this past year. He'd been able to keep it away from his shipmates on the *Esmerelda*—you didn't mix business with pleasure, after all—but eventually the debt piled a bit too high. What was worse was that Pyrig found out he was second mate on the *Esmerelda*, which necessitated a quick and sudden departure. He wasn't about to risk his crewmates, and Pyrig got *nasty* when you owed him money.

Now, though, everything was taken care of. All he had to do was follow orders. It didn't matter if he was killed, because Gora and the kids would be taken care of. If he hadn't taken this job, he would've died anyhow—Pyrig would've killed him. He only hadn't done so up until now because Gobink had convinced Pyrig that, if Gobink was dead, he'd never pay the debt. But after two months of that, Pyrig told him that he'd rather kill him than have to deal with him anymore.

Luckily, the job came along, Pyrig was paid off, and Gobink was promised repeatedly that Gora and the kids would be fine no matter what.

As for the Castle Guard, they didn't even know his name, and they never would. Even if, by some miracle, they figured out he was a sailor, no way that the captain or Forlis would give him up. He'd spread around too much gold for that to happen. Nothing the captain liked better than gold and nothing he hated more than the Guard.

Finally, two Cloaks walked in, briefly letting in light from the outside. It was late afternoon, and for a brief moment, he could see the light from the setting sun over the Forest of Nimvale as seen from the huge window that took up the entirety of the Cloaks' north window.

But after a moment, the door was shut, and he was back in the prison-like room that was worse than an actual prison. He found himself once again facing the elf woman and the human man from the last time.

The human stood near the wall while the elf sat across from him in one of the chairs. The latter said, "Sorry to drag you back up here, but we won't have to keep you long this time."

Folding his arms over his small chest, Gobink said nothing. He had yet to say a single word to the Cloaks, not right after he was caught by that ugly half-elf, not when these two questioned him the first time, and he wouldn't now.

The elf went on: "You see, we don't actually *need* to speak to you anymore. We have you on attempting to murder the king and queen, as well as smuggling a weapon into a gathering hosted by the king and queen. The penalty for the first of those, by the way, is for the perpetrator and for any living member of the perpetrator's family to be boiled in oil. Which rather makes the penalty for the second redundant, but still."

Gobink swallowed, but remained silent. They didn't know his name, so they didn't know his family. They said they'd take care of his family if he did the job, even if the job failed. They said that more than once. Gobink did the job, and so Gora and the kids would be safe.

"So," the elf continued, "we'll be handing you over to the magistrate shortly."

The human finally spoke. "Plus, we gotta send messengers ahead to Zignat."

Turning to the human, the elf pointed at him. "Right! We need to issue warrants for the arrest of Gora, Fralak, Kimbrik, and Sanda."

All of a sudden the room got much hotter. Gobink found it difficult to catch his breath.

Looking back at him, the elf asked, "Is something wrong, Gobink?"

Oh, Xinf protect me, they know my name!

"You—you don't s-scare m-me." Gobink tried to sound tough, but his voice came out weak and reedy to his own ears.

"He speaks!" The human grinned at the elf. "You owe me a copper, Aleta." The human then glanced at Gobink. "I bet her a copper that you'd break soon's we mentioned your wife and kids."

Aleta, the elf, shook her head ruefully. "I thought for sure that you would hold out a little longer."

"Yeah, well, maybe he really does give two shits about his family," the human said with a sneer.

"My family will remain protected. I was *promised*." Gobink was trying as hard to convince himself of this as he was the two Cloaks.

Walking toward the table Gobink sat behind, the human shook his head. "You stupid shitbrain. The moment we found out your name, your family was dead."

"Well, not necessarily, Dru," Aleta said. "They could run."

"Yeah, sure, but to where?"

Aleta rubbed her chin thoughtfully. "Fair point. After all, King Marcus and Queen Marta have a treaty with the Dwarven Curia. So anywhere they go in human or dwarven lands, they'd still be fugitives."

Dru, the human, pointed a finger upward. "Hey, they could go to elf country! It's a mess there, they'd probably be able t'lose themselves with no problem."

Now Aleta was staring at Gobink. He looked away quickly. "I don't know, Dru, he *is* a dwarf. They've never been all that fond of my kind. I'm not sure that Gora and her children would be able to stand it."

"Well, I mean, it's gonna suck no matter what," Dru said. "They'll be on the run. They can't go near any'a their friends — that'll be the first place they'll look."

"True." Aleta nodded. "They'll be totally dependent on strangers. And whatever gold Gobink here sent them. But I suspect they'll burn through that pretty quickly in order to stay one step ahead."

However, the longer this conversation went on, the more Gobink realized that he was being played. "Enough, already."

"Excuse me?" The elven woman had a sweet smile on her face when he said that, which just made Gobink hate her even more.

"Look, you wouldn't even bother telling me all of this if you didn't want something from me."

"You're smarter'n you look," Dru said. He sat down next to the elf. "It's simple. You're boilin' in oil. That ain't changin'. Nothin' we could do about it even if we wanted to. And I gotta tell you? We don't wanna. What's up for grabs, though, is your family."

Gobink didn't like the sound of that at all. "What about my family?"

Aleta leaned forward. "I believe we've outlined very specifically what will happen to your family if events run their course naturally. However, if you can find it within yourself to tell us who the other three conspirators are and who hired you, we would consider exempting your wife and your children from your punishment."

For several seconds, Gobink stared at Aleta. Finally, unable to stand the sight of her, he looked away. Lamely, he said, "I need to think about this."

"Really?" Dru asked. "Soon's we mentioned that your family gets boiled in oil, too, you broke out in a sweat. I don't think there's shit for you t'think about. You don't want 'em to die, do you?"

"My children don't deserve this!" he cried suddenly.

"What," Aleta said, "a father who attempts regicide? You're right, they don't. But you're the one who gave them that. All we're doing is spelling out the consequences."

"Look, I don't give a damn if I die. I was gonna anyhow, but Gora—" He sighed. Dru was right, he didn't have a choice. However, he wasn't stupid. "I want assurances in writing that my family will not be subject to my punishment. It must have the lord and lady's seal on it."

"It'll have Sir Rommett's seal on it," Dru said. "That's the best you're gonna get. And *only* if you give up the other three and the one who hired you."

"All right, but—" He hesitated, fearing he was giving up leverage by admitting what he was about to admit.

However, not saying it and then having it revealed later would be far worse.

"But what?" Aleta prompted.

"I don't know who hired us. I know who paid us, but he was just a flunky, not the boss. And I won't tell you a damn thing about him or the other three until I see that scroll with the seal on it."

Gobink went back to folding his arms, hoping it was as defiant a gesture now as it was when the Cloaks walked in. The only thing that mattered was Gora and their children. If he couldn't protect them, he wasn't worth a damn.

And maybe I'm not worth a damn anyhow, but I won't let them be boiled in oil or force them to live in hiding because I was an idiot.

TEN

THE FIRST TIME TORIN AND DANTHRES SLEPT TOGETHER WAS TWO YEARS INTO their partnership. It was their second midsummer as partners, but that particular year midsummer also coincided with Wiate's Moon Festival—which was at a different time every year. So in addition to the usual parades and celebrations tied to the midsummer arrival of the large golden dragon that encircled the city-state three times, sometimes blew a fireball, and then left, there was also everyone in the demesne who worshipped Wiate, or at least claimed to, dancing and feasting and drinking while wearing bizarre face makeup that represented one of Wiate's Seven Minions.

After working their third consecutive shift, and after breaking up their tenth brawl between some of Wiate's Minions and some midsummer celebrants, they stumbled exhausted back to Torin's apartment, by virtue of its being closer to where they happened to be standing when the shift ended.

Looking back on it eight years later as he lay in his bed with Danthres now, Torin had no recollection of who initiated the sex. It shouldn't have been either of them, as they were both fatigued beyond all reason. Torin hadn't been so bone-weary since the battle at Hobgoblin's Run.

Danthres had dozed off and was now sleeping on her side. She rolled over and slowly opened her eyes to see Torin staring at her. He loved the way the sun reflected off her blond hair. Danthres was nobody's idea of beauty, but her passion was both joyous and uninhibited.

"You look pensive," she muttered.

"Just remembering the first time we did this."

She grinned. It was a playful grin, and Torin was fairly certain that he was the only one who ever saw it. "Ah, yes, when you took advantage of my exhaustion to ravage me."

"As I recall," he said with a mock frown, "*you* took advantage of *my* fatigue."

She sat up next to him, back against the headboard, breasts bouncing delightfully as she settled into that position. Torin was on his side, propped up by his left elbow.

Torin continued. "What I *do* remember clearly was what you said the following morning."

Danthres chuckled and quoted herself. "'This will *never ever* happen again, and if you mention it to *anyone*, I will run you through!'"

"I think you threatened to snap my neck, actually, but either way, the sentiment was assuredly homicidal should I consider the possibility of us ever again sleeping together, or of my discussing it."

Again Danthres smiled. "I never told you this, but—well, I honestly thought that that would be the way to finally be rid of you."

Now Torin sat up straight on the bed. "What do you mean?"

With a sigh, Danthres sunk a bit down against the headboard. "Well, you know I never wanted a partner, and I only barely tolerated you, even after two years. At first, I was furious with myself for being weak and giving in to you. Or making you give in to me, or whatever that actually was that night."

Torin chuckled.

"But after that, I expected that you would be like most men. You'd gloat about it to Nael and Iaian and Linder and Osric and Newcastle. So I told you never to tell anyone and that it wouldn't happen again. I just *knew* that you'd either break and tell one of them anyhow, giving me reason to get rid of you as an untrustworthy partner, or you'd go mad from no longer being able to be with me and you'd quit the partnership."

"Not your most cunning plan, that," Torin said dryly.

"No, it wasn't." Danthres shook her head ruefully. "I kept waiting for you to break, and you just *wouldn't*. You kept your word on both counts. I didn't know about your silly little Myverin ways."

Torin laughed at her teasing tone. The people of Myverin were fairly open about sex, and were more than happy to discuss it in theory, but individual sexual encounters were considered private and not fodder for conversation with anyone not part of said sexual encounter.

Torin had had sex with several men and women before leaving Myverin—something Danthres had said once explained his excellent technique—and carried over this rather casual attitude to Cliff's End. But his upbringing meant he was never even in any danger of fulfilling Danthres's hopes.

Danthres's tone then became quieter. "And then after the Kavan case . . ."

Torin nodded, and reached out to cup her cheek. About a month after the midsummer/moon festival combination, several poor children in Goblin, some orphans, some not, were found with their throats cut open. Danthres had been sure that it had been one of the Jorbin's Way merchants—so sure that she had refused to even consider Torin's alternate theory. But Torin had been correct, and they had arrested Kavan for the killings just as he was about to murder another child.

Danthres invited Torin to her bed that night, both as a thank-you and as a release from the nightmare that the case had been up to that point. They'd been regular bedmates ever since, though both had taken on plenty of other lovers, and Torin himself had gotten into a couple of relationships, though neither of them lasted particularly long. Feira, who was a secretary to Madam Lessa in the castle, had broken it off after Linder died, announcing that she decided she couldn't deal with the uncertainty of his life in the Castle Guard. And Gabin moved back to Treemark to be with his family; Torin owed him a letter.

The timechimes rang six times. Danthres looked at Torin. "We've still got an hour."

"Yes," Torin said bitterly, "for another day of working for an imbecile."

Danthres folded her arms over her breasts. "You know, of the two of us, I expected that I would be the one to be the most pissy about Grovis's promotion." She frowned. "*You* didn't want the job, did you?"

"Goodness, no." Torin shuddered. "My whole reasoning for taking the job of lieutenant ten years ago was that it offered the adventure of soldiering with the intellectual challenges of my upbringing. The job of captain offers neither of those things, and I'm just as happy to avoid them. No, I suppose it's Lord Blayk's reasoning as he told us. Grovis happening to be born to a wealthy family does not entitle him to the captaincy. And Osric's lack of same has nothing to do with his own qualifications." He shook his head. "I just fear that the city-state is being run by someone less sensible, and that doesn't bode well."

"Lady Meerka is sensible enough for both of them." Danthres put a hand on his bare arm. "But honestly? I don't know what else you can do on the Beffel case unless he's actually found. I'm not saying Grovis is right to take you off the case, but he is kind of right in that there's little you can do until he comes forward or one of the shitbrains in Dragon manages to stumble across him."

"Nonsense. We can try to discover who used the Keefda stone. That can lead us to the people who committed the assault."

"Manfred can do that. He's quite capable."

Torin regarded her quizzically. "Really? So now you're back to thinking highly of him?"

Danthres looked away. "He's smart enough. Certainly more so than *Kellan*." She shuddered. "Whatever I may think of Manfred personally, he deserved the promotion. Let him trace that stone. I need your help with Lord Albin's murder."

"Didn't Grovis tell you not to?"

She tilted her head. "Technically, he told me that he wouldn't partner me back with you. But there's no reason why you can't help Kellan and I." She sighed. "Look, you know how much I hate talking to the rich shitbrains. And Kellan's even worse than me—I, at least, can *talk* to them."

"Generally," Torin added with a grin, "in a manner that offends them in every possible way."

"Yes, but at least I can open my mouth! Kellan was useless. *You* can actually speak to the nobility and get answers out of them. I'm not convinced they'll *have* those answers, but I need to find out. Especially with this mysterious meeting of Sir Rommett's."

"It is a world gone mad, isn't it?"

"What do you mean?"

"Grovis is captain, Lord Albin and Hawk are dead, Iaian is retired, and Sir Rommett is actually aiding an investigation rather than hindering it."

Danthres chuckled. "Yes, indeed."

"What did Boneen's peel-back tell you?"

"I'm sorry?" Danthres was leaning forward and staring blankly at Torin.

For his part, Torin was shocked. "Danthres, didn't Boneen do a peel-back?"

"Of what? Lord Albin's body's been burned, so—" She fell back against the headboard. "Shit. I'm an idiot. It didn't even occur to me to send him to the office to do the peel-back." She shook her head. "I'm so used to him showing up at a scene . . ." Looking up at Torin, she snarled. "This wouldn't have happened if we'd been allowed to investigate this properly at the time—*before* Blayk got here and turned the place upside down."

"To be fair, we none of us have been thinking straight."

"Yeah." Danthres pursed her lips. "I'll get Boneen on it first thing today."

"Good." Torin lay down next to her on the bed, resting his head on her shoulder. "So when are you going to tell me about Javian?"

She pushed him off her and shifted away from him. "Who told you about Javian?"

"Initially? You did, when Fanthral said he was on his way. I gather he arrived, mostly based on Manfred informing me at the Chain last night. You were missed there, by the by."

Danthres gave him a wicked grin. "So you said when you found me in your bed last night."

He leaned in to kiss her. It had been a pleasant surprise to return home from a night celebrating Manfred, Kellan, and Aleta's promotions, as well as Iaian's retirement—the old soldier had come out for a final post-shift drink-up—at the Old Ball and Chain to see Danthres already in his apartment, already naked, and already in his bed.

After breaking off the kiss, Torin stared into her large brown eyes. "So what happened with Javian?"

Danthres closed her eyes and again pulled away from him. "I don't particularly want to talk about it."

"I don't particularly care. We got sidetracked by Lord Albin when you dropped it on me that he was the one who kicked you out of Sorlin. Now he's here, and you spent quite a bit of time alone in an interview room with him. Who is he, besides the head of the council?"

"No longer." Danthres sighed and got up from the bed, walking over to stare out the window.

Torin got up and stood behind her, snaking his left arm under her left armpit, and embracing her by placing his hand on her right shoulder. Kissing her neck, he looked out at the view of the sun starting to come up over the city, rays peeking between buildings.

"Fanthral's information was correct. The council voted to disband Sorlin, and the vote carried unanimously. Javian's in Cliff's End to book passage to Saptor Isle to retire. Having talked to him—I suspect he might've done that in any case. After he led the vote to have me removed from Sorlin, he resigned from the chair." She broke out of the embrace and turned to look at Torin. "How much do you know about Sorlin? I remember you'd heard of it when we first met."

"Just stories I heard during the war. I know it's located quite a bit south of here."

Danthres nodded and she moved to lean against the wall. "It's on the Kone Peninsula on the southern coast. The rocks on the coastline are vicious. That's why they settled there—it's impossible to approach by sea without risking getting your boat destroyed, and the land approaches are all uphill."

"Very defensible."

"Very necessary—the intent of Sorlin was to be a sanctuary for people who violated elven purity laws, after all."

Torin nodded. He considered prompting her again, but she was actually talking, so he let her tell the story at her own pace.

"When I was a girl, there were three of us who were inseparable: me, Elsthar Javian, and Lilanthria." She actually smiled, then. "Tharri, Thressa, and Lil. We did everything together, the three of us. All half-breeds, but Tharri—Javian—was the only one whose parents were with us. The Javians raised Lil and I as their own, though. It was a wonderful place to live—probably as much a paradise for me as Myverin was for you. More so, really, because unlike you, I'd seen the world outside. For the first few years of my life, my mother and I lived on the run, after my father was killed. We were on our way to Sorlin when she grew ill, but she refused to rest, forcing herself to make it all the way south. She died when we arrived, despite the best efforts of the healers. The Javians had already taken Lil in—she was the product of a human soldier raping an elven prisoner. Her mother killed her rapist when she escaped, and made it to Sorlin, where she died in childbirth. Both our mothers—her elven one, my human one—came to Sorlin because it was a place where everyone lived in peace. Our paramount law was always that disruptions would not be permitted. From the moment you entered Sorlin's borders, you were told that the first law of Sorlin was that anyone who disrupted the society would be cast out."

Danthres looked away and then went back to the bed. Torin slowly moved to sit next to her.

"Tharri was over a decade older than me, so he was already being groomed for the council when I arrived in Sorlin. By the time I was a teenager, he became head of it — he was a natural-born leader, truly. He and Lil also wed. We joked that it was the Elf Queen's worst nightmare: two halfbreeds marrying. They even planned to breed."

Danthres fell silent for a moment. Torin decided to prompt her to continue. "I take it they were unable to?"

She shook her head. "One day the council was debating some point of law or other. It was going on forever, so Lil and I decided to take a walk along the coast. It was a favorite pastime of ours when Tharri was busy with council business, walking along the rocks, getting sprayed by the spume, enjoying the view of the Garamin — something we'd done a thousand times before."

She took a deep breath before continuing. Torin put his arm around her, and Danthres absently reached up to hold the hand that was now draped over her shoulder.

"It had been a beautiful day when we started, but a rainstorm came out of nowhere. That happens a lot that far south — the rain usually passed quickly. So we kept walking, but this was a nastier storm than usual. There was lightning and thunder. A bolt of lightning hit — hit the ground in front of us. We both lost our footing. I — I managed to grab a tree root with one hand, but all Lil had to grab was a piece of wet rock. I reached out for Lil with my other hand, but I couldn't reach her. I tried, Torin, I tried *so hard*, but she was too far, and then she lost her grip and . . ."

In ten years, Torin had never seen Danthres in quite this emotional state. She'd shed tears in his presence, though those occasions were rare, but this was the first time he saw her on the brink of out-and-out crying.

But she didn't. Instead, she tensed up and said, "That was it. She was gone. It was just a stupid accident, but I refused to accept that. I spent every day standing before the council trying to get them to investigate the matter, trying to find out if someone had cast a spell to bring about a nastier storm, to see if someone had made the rocks particularly wet to make it harder to walk on . . ."

"You were disruptive," Torin said quietly.

Danthres nodded. "Tharri was right when we talked yesterday. He told me that the council didn't have a choice, and I didn't really give them one. I was impossible, because I refused to accept that someone I loved as much as I loved her could die from something so—so *stupid*." She shook her head and barked a bitter laugh. "My father was killed by an angry mob of elves, and my mother and I lived on the run for a year before we made it to Sorlin. I was hunted just because of who my parents were—you would think that I'd have been well versed in the notion of the unfairness of the world. Yet I couldn't accept *that*. I couldn't accept that my dearest friend, my sister in all but blood, was dead. And I couldn't save her, and I couldn't avenge her."

A tear slowly trickled down her cheek. Torin wrapped his arms around her, and she buried her face in his neck.

They stayed that way for quite some time.

ELEVEN

By the time Danthres and Torin finally made it to the castle, it was three-quarters of an hour past when the timechimes rang seven. That was late even by Torin's usual tardy standards, and if Danthres actually gave a damn what Grovis thought of her, she might have tried to get him to move his ass faster.

Sergeant Jonas glared at them as they came in. "You're both late."

"We were already aware of that, Jonas, thank you," Danthres said.

Manfred and Kellan were sitting at their desks talking to each other. Jonas had assigned them to Iaian and Grovis's old desks. "Glad you're finally here," Manfred said.

Torin was staring at Manfred's sword belt. "You still have the surplus sword."

"Yes." Manfred sounded cranky. "Molano told me it'd be ready first thing, but when I stopped by on my way here, she said she got backed up with orders from the castle."

"What kind of orders?" Torin asked.

Manfred shrugged. "She didn't say, and she was running around like a crazy woman, so I didn't get to ask. Why?"

"Just curious." Torin sat at his desk. "In any event, did we miss anything?"

Kellan said, "Last night, I asked around about Del Francit."

Danthres frowned for a moment, then remembered that he was someone Sir Palrik mentioned. "What about him?"

"If he had any friends, nobody knew about 'em. His own father disowned him and kicked him out onto the streets. I can't see nobody avengin' him by killin' Lord Albin."

"That was always a long shot." Danthres let out a breath.

Jonas shuffled some parchments around. There were times when Danthres believed that they were all blank and he just had them in his hands to make himself look busy. "Aleta and Dru are talking to the magistrate. They're trying to work out a deal with Gobink, and they need his approval."

Danthres found herself unable to be surprised that the Shranlaseth bitch and the still-mourning Dru had messed this one up. "They're making a *deal* with that shit-sucking troll?"

"In a manner of speaking," Jonas said. "He's still getting the full punishment for what he did — what's being negotiated is the fate of his family. He's willing to give up his conspirators in exchange for his wife and children not being boiled in oil."

That got Danthres to relent. "That's a disgusting law in any case."

"Agreed," Torin said. "One cannot hold someone's family responsible for one's actions."

Manfred shrugged. "Well, the king and queen can. It's one of their laws, not the lord and lady's."

"It's still disgusting." Danthres looked past Manfred at her new partner. "C'mon, Kellan, we need to ask Boneen for something. You can get your first experience of being complained to by a wizard older than your grandfather."

Kellan chuckled as he rose from his desk. "Ain't gonna be the first, I can tell you that. I found a dead gnome named Djili in an alley a while back. When the M.E. showed up, I didn't hear the end of it from him for an hour. Only break I got was when he cast the peel-back."

"Which lieutenant caught that case?" Danthres asked.

Now Kellan looked nervous. "Er, well, no one did. I handled it. That was back when you an' Lieutenant ban Wyvald were doin' the Cynnis murder, an' the other detectives had big cases, too."

Danthres was about to get angry, but then she remembered the Cynnis murder. It was at the same time that Iaian and Grovis were looking into corruption in Mermaid Precinct and Dru and Hawk were looking into a fraudulent Temisan priest. All three were politically sensitive cases. Arra Cynnis was a girl of noble birth about to marry into the Grovis family, the lord and lady were on a fight-corruption kick, and the Temisan bishopric was very influential. Anything that came up during that awful period was left to the guards.

She supposed that this Djili bastard could've done worse than to have Kellan looking into her murder. Not *a lot* worse, of course . . .

They proceeded through the corridor adjacent to the squadroom to the staircase that led down to Boneen's lair in the basement.

However, when they got to the bottom of the stairs, the door to the sanctum had been removed. Looking through the now-open doorframe, Danthres saw that there was nothing in the space at all. The shelves, the tables, the potions, the crystals—they were all gone.

Danthres stared at the empty room for several seconds.

Kellan stared at her. "I'm guessin' that this ain't usual for Boneen's place?"

"Your grasp of the blindingly obvious remains strong as ever, Kellan." Danthres spoke in an unnecessarily snide voice, but right now she cared about her partner's feelings not in the least. She stormed past him. "C'mon, we need to talk to our *esteemed* captain."

Without bothering to see if Kellan followed her, Danthres went upstairs and back to the squadroom, making a beeline for Grovis's office.

Torin was talking with Manfred about something, but he looked up at Danthres's arrival. "That was fast."

"Boneen's gone."

"What?" Torin stood up at his desk. "What do you mean 'gone'?"

"Just what I said," Danthres said tightly.

"The whole room was *completely* empty," Kellan put in. "Didn't even have a door or nothin'."

"That bodes ill."

Manfred said, "We could just be getting a new magickal examiner."

"Only one way to find out." Danthres went into the captain's office to find Grovis reading over a scroll. Kellan didn't follow her in, the coward, but Torin did.

Grovis looked up. "What is it the pair of you want?"

"What happened to Boneen? We need him to cast a peel-back on Lord Albin's office."

Getting to his feet, Grovis said primly, "I'm afraid that the Castle Guard will no longer be employing the services of a magickal examiner. If you had actually shown up for roll call as you are supposed to, you would have found that out."

Torin put his hands on his hips. "You couldn't have mentioned it at roll call—Manfred and Kellan were unaware of it."

"Of course I didn't mention it," Grovis said, "but you would have during roll call, at which point I would have saved you a trip downstairs."

"Why in the lord and lady's name have we gotten rid of the M.E.?" Danthres realized her voice was carrying, but she also realized that she didn't give a damn.

"You have, in fact, Danthres, put your finger on it regarding the lord and lady. It is Lord Blayk who has released Boneen from his duties."

Before Danthres could shout again, Torin jumped in. "Did he give a reason for this imbecilic course of action?"

"The lord of the demesne believes, quite rightly in my opinion, that, as useful as the magickal examiner is, it's a waste of a wizard's valuable time to be spent as an errand boy for the Castle Guard."

Danthres screamed this time. "You shitbrained *idiot*!"

"Mind your tone, Lieutenant!"

"No, *Captain*, I don't think I will!"

Torin stepped forward, interpolating himself between Danthres and Grovis. Only then did Danthres realize that she had moved forward in a threatening manner and was almost nose to nose with Grovis.

"I will not be spoken to this way!" Grovis shouted.

After giving Danthres a nasty look, Torin regarded Grovis seriously. "Captain, with all due respect, the Brotherhood of Wizards *also* thinks the M.E. is a waste of time."

"All the more reason to be rid of it, then, don't you think?" Grovis asked snidely.

"The only reason the Brotherhood agreed to assign Boneen was because Lord Albin blackmailed them into it, in exchange for our keeping secret about the fact that one of their most respected wizards was a murderer three times over."

Grovis's mouth fell open into one of his classic fish expressions and his eyes goggled. "What?"

Danthres had stepped back a bit and managed to almost compose herself. "It was Torin's and my first case together. When it was over, and we'd gotten a wizard named Myk Dourti to confess, the Brotherhood gave us Boneen so they could handle Dourti themselves."

Torin shook his head. "You've just given away one of the most important resources the Guard has for no benefit except to toady to wizards who won't appreciate it."

"Well, you could say we're doing them a favor . . ." Grovis sounded dubious even as he said it.

"Yes," Danthres said snidely, "because the Brotherhood is known for their generosity."

"I—" Grovis gestured helplessly.

"You've crippled our effectiveness and made it that much harder to solve our cases. Well done, Grovis." Danthres actually patted his shoulder in a mock-friendly gesture. "And only your third day on the job. Imagine how much damage you'll do in a week!"

With that, she turned and left Grovis's office, Torin following only after giving the captain one last doleful look.

Danthres fell more than sat in her chair and stared angrily at the scrolls on her desk. "I'm this close to quitting."

"And what will you do then?" Torin asked as he sat at his desk, abutting hers.

"I don't know. Maybe go with Javian to Saptor."

Torin snorted derisively. "And what would you do after a month when the novelty wears off and you're bored to death?"

"You're right, I should definitely stay here so Grovis and Blayk can make me crazy enough to kill someone. Then I'll be hanged and put out of my misery."

Kellan walked over to sit on the edge of Torin's desk. Under other circumstances, she might have been amused by the fact that he wasn't suicidal enough to try doing that on Danthres's desk. "Well, until you actually go on your homicidal rampage, what do we do next?"

Torin looked at Manfred. "Can you make some inquiries regarding that Keefda stone that was used in the Beffel case?"

Manfred frowned. "I thought we were off that."

"Whatever inclination I may have had to do as Grovis says was removed by our most recent conversation," Torin said dryly. "I want to know where that stone came from. Check all the magick shops and see who might have such a thing. Start with the ones in Dragon, they're the ones most likely to have high-ticket items such as that. And see if you can find anything out about Beffel."

"Okay. What'll you be doing?"

Smiling at Danthres, Torin said, "Aiding my fellow detectives with my ability to speak to the nobility without strangling them or quivering in fear."

"I don't quiver in fear!" Kellan cried out, standing upright.

Danthres found herself grinning quite against her will. "It certainly looked like quivering to me." She also stood. "You go with him, Kellan, you might learn something."

"Where will you be?" Kellan asked.

"Grovis said that it was a decree from the lord and lady that released Boneen from his obligations as M.E., but I suspect that it's only the lord who made that decree. What's more, I doubt the lady knew a damn thing about it."

"You plan to talk to her?"

Danthres shrugged. "She specifically asked me to take on this case. I think I'm completely justified in talking to her to fill her in—and telling her how the lack of an M.E. is complicating the case."

TWO HOURS LATER, DANTHRES FINALLY GOT IN TO SEE LADY MEERKA. SHE had been in a meeting with some bankers. Danthres considered the efficacy of barging in on the meeting, but given that the largest bank in Cliff's End was owned by Grovis's father, that was probably not the best idea. The new captain was already making her life miserable, there wasn't much point in giving him more ammunition by having dear old Daddy bitch about that half-elf detective who interrupted his important meeting with Lady Meerka and could Amilar be a good son and fire her, please?

That would be the perfect ending to this week, wouldn't it?

When the lady did arrive, she was surprised to see Danthres there. "Has your investigation borne fruit, Lieutenant?"

"Not exactly."

"That is a very evasive answer, Lieutenant. Please, come into my chambers and we will discuss it more directly."

Danthres followed her into the office, which was just as well organized as it had been the last time she set foot in it.

"I hope you weren't kept waiting long. I was discussing the new security procedures that are now required by law for all banks to have. Harcort Grovis was rather tiresome on the subject of how expensive they were, but that awful business that led to your Lieutenant Hawk being killed could have been avoided if the banks had proper protection. I will not have the citizenry's money so vulnerable."

As she had nothing specific to say in response to that, Danthres didn't reply, waiting for a better opening to explain her own problem.

"The meeting might have ended sooner, but Harcort would make excuses for his behavior. It isn't as if those excuses mattered. For one thing, I'm not interested in them. The events already happened and attempting to assign blame now is a frivolous endeavor. For another, the excuses weren't even good ones, as they did nothing to explain why he neglected to inform me of their discontinuation of the security protocols they had in place." She finally sat in her chair, having spent the entirety of the tirade pacing behind it. "My apologies, Lieutenant. You did not come to my office to listen to my complaints with the banking bureaucracy. Please explain what you meant by 'not exactly.'"

"As you probably know, our usual method for investigating a crime begins with an investigation of the scene where the crime occurred. The detectives do a visual inspection, of course, but our best tool for that portion of the process was the M.E."

"Why did you use the past tense when describing the magickal examiner?" The lady's tone, Danthres noticed, was harsh, which confirmed what she had suspected.

"Your son dismissed Boneen from his position."

"For what reason?"

"You'll have to ask Lord Blayk, my lady." Danthres added a shrug. She had briefly toyed with the notion of giving the reasons Grovis did, but it served her purpose more to have the lady think they were being kept in the dark. "All I know is that we went to ask Boneen to cast the peel-back—"

"I'm sorry?"

Danthres blinked. "Er, the Inanimate Residue Spell. We call it a 'peel-back.'"

"I can't imagine why, that's not what it's called."

After a brief hesitation, Danthres soldiered on. "In any case, when we went to Boneen's workspace in the basement, it was cleared out. Captain Grovis informed us that he'd been dismissed. And we wanted him to cast the, ah, the Inanimate Residue Spell on your late husband's sitting room. But that option was taken away from us."

Lady Meerka pursed her lips. "Strictly speaking, of course, my son's actions were completely within his purview. As he reminded me when I last called you into my office, the Castle Guard is under his control, not mine. I'm afraid I cannot censure him for this action directly. It is very peculiar, and quite damaging, though. I do wonder what his reasoning was."

It took all of Danthres's will power to keep from snarling. Especially now, the lady of the demesne was too valuable an ally to risk her alienating.

As soon as Danthres had that thought, she was utterly appalled with herself. *I'm starting to think politically.* True, it was only with regard to Lady Meerka—the rest of the nobility could go hang as far as she was concerned—but it was still an odd feeling.

"Is there anything else, Lieutenant?"

"We questioned several of the sirs and madams here in the castle, but they weren't particularly helpful. We're still talking to them, though, so something may come up. Also, Sir Rommett did mention that he was having a meeting with Lord Albin the day he died—but Sir Rommett had no idea what it was about. You wouldn't happen to know, would you?"

"Oh goodness, no. I long ago stopped attempting to keep track of my husband's meetings. I'm sorry, I don't know a thing about that. And my son has dismissed his father's secretary, but perhaps you can find her."

"I'm afraid not." Danthres quickly explained that Lord Albin's former secretary was on a boat somewhere in the Garamin and unreachable.

She also realized that she had only one card left to play, but it was a risky one, as it would put her word against that of Lord Blayk.

"My lady," she said hesitantly, "there is one other aspect of this case that I feel needs to be mentioned."

"Oh? What is that, Lieutenant?"

"After you tasked me and Lieutenant Kellan with investigating your husband's death, Lord Blayk took me aside and told me it was a fool's errand. He asked that I only do a perfunctory investigation, just enough to satisfy you."

"Why would he do that?"

"He believes that Lord Albin died of an illness."

Meerka rolled her eyes. "Why should we be bound by what he *believes*? The point of the investigation is to find out the truth. Perhaps he *did* die of an illness—I'm the first to admit that the word of a house faerie is hardly conclusive—but it is, at the very least, the basis of trying to determine the reality of what happened. Blayk has always been more interested in what might be and what he believes than in the evidence of his own eyes. I told him as a boy that it would be his downfall if he didn't hew to facts rather than beliefs." She looked straight at Danthres. "Are you doing as my son says?"

"I am investigating Lord Albin's death, my lady." She let herself smile. "I'm afraid I'm not really capable of doing anything in a perfunctory manner. When I look into a death, I do so thoroughly."

"Good." Meerka actually smiled back. It wasn't a particularly pleasant expression on her. "I've admired you for some time, Lieutenant. You're quite an asset to the Castle Guard. I'm glad Osric was able to see that and promote you when he did."

"Thank you, my lady. We will continue our work, and I will keep you apprised."

"Yes, see that you do. In fact, I hereby authorize you, for the duration of this investigation, to report directly to me any updates in the case. I prefer not to bypass the chain of command so aggressively, but my son's recalcitrance gives me little option."

Danthres rose. "As you say, my lady."

"In fact, we shall formalize it. You are to report to me at the end of each of your shifts until the case is closed. Not today, since there's only half the day left, but starting tomorrow."

Giving the lady a small bow, Danthres said, "Thank you, my lady."

She then left the office with as large a grin as she was capable of. Indeed, it was possibly the first time she'd ever grinned while in the western wing of the castle. For the first time since Hawk's death, Danthres felt like she might actually have some measure of control over the world again . . .

BY THE TIME TORIN AND KELLAN APPROACHED SIR PALRIK'S OFFICE, HE WAS getting well and truly frustrated.

First Sir and Madam Wint couldn't speak, as they had several new requisitions from the lord and lady's office: reinforcing the docklands, repairing the long-disused portcullis on the castle, and an addition onto the castle to serve as what the requisition referred to as "temporary housing."

Sir Lio couldn't speak because he'd been asked to write a detailed report on all the methods of entering Cliff's End and how secure they were.

Madam Roth, the taxation minister, couldn't speak because Lord Blayk had requested a change in the tax structure for the aristocracy, with payments increased and now coming twice a month instead of monthly.

Sir Latzko, the armory minister, couldn't speak because he had to supervise a full annotated inventory of the castle's arms and armament and also write a report on the feasibility of switching the Castle Guard personnel from leather armor to metal armor.

As they approached Sir Palrik's office, Kellan said, "When Lieuten—er, when Danthres and I talked to this gentleman yesterday, he said he served with you?"

Torin nodded. "When I met him during the war, I had no idea he was a member of the nobility It wasn't until I came to Cliff's End and he was referred to as 'Sir Palrik' that I found out He gave no impression of aristocracy as a soldier, certainly."

"He didn't seem to have much to do, really. Everyone else we talked to had some kinda function, but he was just sittin' around smokin' a pipe."

"Yes, well, there really isn't much need for a chief military advisor when there's no war. I've always assumed that Lord Albin considered the position ceremonial, and gave it to him in recognition of his service."

"Makes sense."

The pair of them arrived at the office only to find a familiar-looking dwarf hanging a Fjorm axe on the wall of the office and no sign of Sir Palrik.

Torin was stunned. "General Ubàrlig?"

"Yes?" The dwarf turned to face them. "Ah, Lieutenant ban Wyvald. A pleasure to see you again." He glanced at Kellan. "I'm afraid we haven't met, have we, Lieutenant?"

"No, sir." Kellan stepped forward and offered a gloved hand. "I'm Arn Kellan, and it's an honor to meet you, sir."

Ubàrlig returned the handshake. "The honor is mine, Lieutenant."

"If I may ask," Torin said slowly, "why are you hanging your axe in Sir Palrik's office?"

"Because this is *not* Sir Palrik's office any longer. Lord Blayk asked me to take over his job."

Torin straightened and blinked. "Excuse me?"

"I'm Cliff's End's new military advisor." Ubàrlig let out a long sigh. "I must confess, I didn't expect the offer, and I came very close to declining it. But my days of adventuring are truly long behind me. With

Gan, Olthar, Mari, and Nari all dead, with Genero in trouble with the bishopric again, and Bogg having gone home, I realized that it might be wise to settle somewhere."

Kellan was practically agog. "I'm sure that Cliff's End will be a better place for your service, sir."

However, Torin was more concerned about the case. "You wouldn't happen to know where Sir Palrik went?"

Ubàrlig shrugged. "Back to his home, I would think. I don't know, the office was empty when I arrived this morning. Now if you'll excuse me, Lieutenants, unless there's anything else, I have several messages to send out to some old comrades."

"No, that *is* all," Torin said grimly. "We have questions regarding Lord Albin's death, and you were in Velessa when that occurred, so I'm afraid you won't be of much help. Thank you for your time."

Torin turned and left quickly, leaving the dwarf to decorate his new office. Kellan blurted out, "It was truly an honor, sir!" before running to catch up to him.

"Let's go back to the squadroom," Torin said quietly.

"I can't *believe* that." Kellan was grinning like a child. "That's *Ubàrlig*! He fought with Gan Brightblade against Mitos the Mighty!"

For a moment, Torin considered telling Kellan just what a pain in the ass Ubàrlig had been, first by obstructing his and Danthres's investigation into his comrades' deaths, then again when they almost assaulted two people because they happened to once work for Mitos. But the young man's enthusiasm was infectious, and besides, sometimes it was better to think of heroes as heroes instead of people. People more often disappointed.

And these past days had been filled with too many disappointments as it was.

TWELVE

W HEN L ORD B LAYK HAD INFORMED A MILAR G ROVIS THAT HE WAS BEING promoted to captain, he was utterly stunned. For one thing, he never truly expected that Osric would willingly retire. He had always struck Grovis as the type who would continue to work until the day he fell over dead on his desk — probably while in the midst of yelling at one of the detectives for some imagined offense or other.

The lord of the demesne's reasons for doing so were eminently sensible, of course. Grovis had many issues with the structure of the Castle Guard, including the fact that a commoner served as its head. It was Grovis's considered opinion that an unkempt soldier, no matter how talented, wasn't truly suited to the role of leading men and women of intellect, as detectives needed to be.

Still, it hadn't been how he expected things to go. He'd anticipated only to serve as a detective for at best another few months before Daddy finally let him work at the bank. His father, for reasons known only to himself and Ghandurha, had decreed that his son Amilar needed to spend some time serving in the Castle Guard in order to make a man of him. Grovis had thought that nature had taken care of that already, but Daddy disagreed.

At first, of course, the promotion had been wonderful. He was in a position more worthy of his station. Lord Blayk had been kind enough to encourage Iaian to retire — while Grovis had come to respect his erstwhile partner over their time together, he was a hidebound old fool who needed getting rid of. By bringing in new blood such as Aleta and Manfred and Kellan, Lord Blayk was giving Grovis a chance to mold the detective squad in his own image.

But once the initial joy had worn off, he couldn't help but notice that there was very little molding he was going to be allowed to do. Lord

Blayk had dictated who would partner with whom, had instituted policy changes without consulting with Grovis, including the dismissal of Boneen, and generally didn't seem interested in letting Grovis be in any way involved in the decision making. Upon his arrival in the squadroom this morning, besides the news about the M.E., he'd also been informed that the sergeants in the four precincts within the city-state were to schedule weapons testing for all the guards under their command. Grovis couldn't imagine that Lord Albin would have instituted such a change without at least discussing it with Osric first, yet here was his son not giving Grovis even the courtesy of a conversation.

A knock came at the door of his office, and he looked up, fearing it would be Torin or Danthres. The pair of them were indeed the finest detectives in the squadroom, but since Lord Albin's death, they'd been disgustingly disagreeable. Grovis intended to give them a very firm talking-to on the subject, once they calmed down a bit. Trying it now would just result in their hitting him with even more disrespect, and Grovis didn't think he could bear that. Worse, it would cause morale issues; the guards and the other detectives all looked up to Danthres and Torin, and Grovis had learned in his tenure in the Guard that alienating those below you before you've gained their respect would only cause more issues down the line.

However, when he looked upward at the doorway to his office, he saw Dru and Aleta instead. "Ah, come in, please. What progress have you made with Gobink?"

"Some, but not nearly enough." Dru sat down in one of the guest chairs.

Aleta, Grovis noted, waited until Dru was seated before sitting as well. "Once the magistrate agreed to enforce Sir Rommett's request that any punishment for his wife and children be waived, Gobink was *very* forthcoming. He gave us the names of the three who worked with him, and said they were staying at the Dog and Duck."

"Ah, good," Grovis said, folding his hands on the desk, "so when will you be going to the inn to find them?"

Dru and Aleta exchanged a confused glance. "We already been," the former finally said. "Olaf said they checked out right after the funeral."

Grovis pursed his lips. "That's not good. Did Gobink at least provide descriptions in addition to the names?"

Aleta stared at him for a moment. "He didn't need to, sir, I saw them quite clearly at the funeral."

"Ah, yes, of course." He forgot that the elven woman was a former member of the Shranlaseth. While Grovis wasn't sure how much he heard was fanciful stories and how much was truth, he was certain that she would provide a good description of the would-be assassins.

"We went to the precincts to provide those descriptions," Aleta said.

"Yeah," Dru added, "and they didn't exactly fill us with joy."

"What do you mean?" Grovis asked, confused.

Dru leaned forward. "We went t'Dragon first, 'cause that's closest to the Dog an' Duck, and Grint told us that he'd do his best, but he's got a quarter of his people off doin' weapons qualifications all shift, an' that's goin' on for a few days. The rest of his guys're on crowd control."

"Well, of course." Grovis nodded appreciably. "The city-state has been quite crowded."

"But, with respect, sir, it isn't." Aleta, Grovis noted, actually sounded respectful when using that phrase, which made her depressingly unique among the detectives, who generally used that phrase to precede a sentiment that was wholly without respect. "The number of people on the streets has dropped precipitously since the funeral. Mermaid is still a bit of a mess because of all the people leaving on boats, but Dragon and Goblin don't have any kind of crowd-control issues."

"But Grint an' Markon," Dru said, referring to the sergeants in charge of Dragon and Goblin Precincts, respectively, "both got told they hadda keep doin' crowd control even though there ain't no crowds. Gonna make it hard for 'em t'look for folks, y'know?"

"And Sergeant Arron received the same instructions." Aleta gave a quick glance to Dru, who nodded. "Sir, it makes no sense to put the guards of Unicorn Precinct on crowd control. But all four sergeants were given the same instructions, to forego the usual patrols for crowd control, and to also make sure that all their guards were tested in the next three days for weapons proficiency."

"Those are the orders they were given, and they are the orders they shall follow," Grovis said primly.

"Sir, excuse me, but—" Aleta hesitated. "You said 'orders they were given.' Does that mean *you* didn't give those orders?"

"No, of course not, it was Lord Blayk." As soon as Grovis said the words, he regretted them. "But it wouldn't matter if I had! The chain of command must be respected, of course."

"Right." Dru was giving Grovis a dubious expression, which he didn't appreciate.

Deciding to ignore it, he asked, "Did you learn anything else about the conspirators? Such as, for example, who hired them?"

Dru shook his head. "No names. All he could tell us was that it was a gnome with a lisp. Oh, and the gnome was from Iaron."

"But the gnome never gave his name," Aleta said, "and the best Gobink could do for a description was the lisp."

A pagegirl stuck her head into the captain's office. "'Scuse me, Cap'n Osric, sir? Oops, sorry, I meant t'say Cap'n Grovis, sir?"

Grovis let out a very loud sigh. He supposed that sort of thing wasn't going to stop any time soon. "Yes?"

"Lord Albin wants t'see ya. Oops, sorry, I meant t'say Lord Blayk wants t'see ya."

"Of course." Grovis supposed that having the girl also forget who was lord of the demesne now made it a bit easier to deal with her not remembering who was captain of the guard. He got up from his chair and led Dru, Aleta, and the pagegirl out of the office. To the former two, he said, "Please keep me posted on your progress, Lieutenants. We must find out who's at the heart of this conspiracy."

Grovis then followed the pagegirl toward the squadroom's doorway, just as Torin and Kellan were coming through it.

"Ah, Grovis," Torin said. "We've just been talking to some of the nobles about Lord Albin."

"Why are *you* involved in that case?"

Torin smiled sweetly. "Well, you *did* take me off the Beffel case, and Danthres and Kellan felt I might have more luck speaking to the aristocrats."

Grovis had to concede that point. Kellan was an unknown quantity, but Danthres had never had the knack of speaking to those in power, whereas Torin was one of the most diplomatic people Grovis had ever met. So he decided not to chastise him, and instead simply asked, "What did you find out?"

"Nothing good. Most of the aristocrats are busy with new tasks they've been assigned by Lord Blayk."

Shrugging, Grovis said, "Well, that's to be expected. He is looking to make his mark on Cliff's End."

"It's more than that. There's a pattern to everything he's doing." Torin started enumerating points on his fingers. "He's raising taxes on the aristocracy, and also collecting more often. He's looking to increase the security of the port and the castle, both structurally and philosophically, and he's ordered more arms and armor for the castle. He's having a barracks constructed, and he's gotten rid of Sir Palrik, replacing him with General Ubàrlig, who has been tasked with hiring mercenaries." Having run out of fingers on his right hand, Torin folded his arms over his chest. "On top of that, he's been encouraging many of the older guards to retire early by vesting their pensions prematurely — it isn't just Iaian, he's also gone after Mannit, Rob Wirrn, Ungrilig, and Hanna Serviling."

"What do you make of all this?" Grovis asked, who honestly didn't see the connection.

Torin gave him an almost pitying look. "It's obvious; he's putting Cliff's End on a war footing."

That confused Grovis, as he wasn't aware of any wars brewing — and his family usually kept up on these things, as the ebb and flow of war and peace often had a direct impact on the banking industry.

But before he could question Torin more thoroughly about it, the pagegirl said, "Lord Blayk said to bring you right away, sir!"

"Yes, of course." He allowed himself to be led by the girl through the hallways of the castle to Lord Blayk's office. Grovis noticed that several of the statues had been removed, and that workers were putting tapestries up on the walls. Grovis found them all to be tacky and had preferred the sculptures that Lord Albin had decorated the castle with. It gave the place a more respectable feel.

To Grovis's surprise, the lord of the demesne was alone in his office. It was the first time since Lord Albin's funeral that Grovis had seen him without the gnome assistant who seemed to be attached to his hip.

"You wished to see me, my lord?"

"Not especially, but seeing you is the only method by which I may speak to you." Lord Blayk tugged on the end of his moustache. "I have been told by several people that Lieutenant ban Wyvald was asking questions of the nobility regarding my father's death, accompanied by Lieutenant Kellan."

Grovis struggled to come up with a reason he could give the lord as to why Torin had inserted himself into Danthres and Kellan's case that he would find acceptable, but Blayk was still talking.

"I believe my instructions were quite clear on how I wished the detectives in your squad to be partnered. Ban Wyvald was to be paired with Lieutenant Manfred, and Lieutenant Tresyllione with Kellan, and it was the latter two who were assigned to investigate my father's death." He shook his head and looked down at one of the many slates on his desk. "I have no idea *what* Mother was thinking, but that is neither here nor there. It is bad enough that Tresyllione and Kellan are wasting their time investigating a death by illness, I will not have ban Wyvald doing likewise. Please place him back with Manfred where he belongs."

Every instinct in Grovis's body told him to say something deferential and positive, something that would indicate his fealty and desire to continue to fulfill the wishes of the lord of the demesne. This despite the revelation that Lord Blayk didn't think investigating his father's death was worthy of the detective squad's attention.

So it came as rather a surprise to Grovis to hear the following words come out of his mouth: "I was under the impression, my lord, that the job description of captain of the guard was to actually *be* the captain of the guard."

That got Lord Blayk to look up from his slate. "What are you blathering about, Grovis?"

"The allocation of the lieutenants under my command falls under *my* purview. I am, of course, more than happy to accept your recommendations as to how that might best be accomplished, but if you wish for me to do my job, I need to be able to *do* it."

Blayk leaned forward and stared intently at him. "Your job, Grovis, is to do as I tell you to do without question. If I tell you to jump, the only question I expect to hear from you is an inquiry as to how high, is that clear, *Captain*?"

"My lord, I'm sorry, but I cannot do my job if I'm seen to be little more than your mouthpiece. You said you wanted a man of breeding in the job."

"I wanted a man of breeding because aristocrats understand their place in the grand scheme of things, Grovis. *Your* place is to do as *I* say. I have very specific plans for this city-state, and your job—your only job—is to ease the implementation of them. If you cannot do that, you may return to your father's bank and I will find someone who can do the job I appointed them to do."

Before Grovis could even think of a possible reply to that — especially in light of what Torin had told him — the gnome assistant walked in, carrying three slates. Without a word, he handed them to Blayk.

The lord studied them, tugging on his mustache some more. "Are these all the figures?" he asked the gnome.

"Yeth, thir, abtholutely."

Grovis felt the digested remains of the pastries Sergeant Jonas's wife had made that morning start to rumble and creep up into his throat.

He swallowed loudly and stammered for a moment, clearing his throat audibly.

Blayk looked disgusted and sneered at him. "That will be all, Grovis. But if I hear of ban Wyvald wandering the castle asking about Father's death, there will be trouble, do I make myself clear?"

"Absolutely, my lord. If you'll excuse me."

Grovis practically ran out of the office.

THIRTEEN

IAIAN STEPPED ONTO SANDY BROOK WAY AND STARED UP AT THE SKY. THE late afternoon sun was casting shadows onto the thoroughfare. It was a beautiful fall day, not too hot, not too cold, much less humidity than usual, and just generally wonderful.

Of course, as far as Iaian was concerned, it could've been a blizzard in midwinter and he'd have been happier than a troll in sheep shit.

At last, he was free. No more squeezing himself into ill-fitting armor and uncomfortable boots. No more sword banging against his leg. No more dealing with a parade of imbeciles one after the other. No more Osric making his life a living torture. No more Danthres being her usual bitchy self.

Best of all, no more Grovis.

Instead, he got to implement his retirement plan two years early. The money he'd hoarded from various and sundry payoffs and bribes and such had gone to pay for one of the new houses on Oak Way. Iaian had even gotten it cheap, too, since the person who'd commissioned the house decided he didn't want to live in Cliff's End after the dragon burned down one of the other nearby houses during midsummer, and so was willing to let it go for a song. (Okay, a complicated song in a minor key, but still . . .) He set his wife up there where she could live out the rest of her life as an upper-middle-class woman of leisure, and need never see Iaian again, which made her happy.

Meanwhile, he took a small apartment here on Sandy Brook Way, the location of most of the bordellos in the city-state.

He had slept in this morning, and spent most of the afternoon in the arms of two lovely women named . . . Actually, Iaian couldn't recall their names, but they were definitely lovely. And energetic.

Tomorrow, I think I stick with one. I'm getting too old for threesomes.

Everything was perfect in Iaian's world.

Which made the appearance of Amilar Grovis standing outside the door that led to his second-story flat rather irritating.

"Shit, I thought I was done with your fish-faced ass, boy."

Grovis had his arms folded, and he was tut-tutting disapprovingly. "I should have known. I went to your place of residence, but your landlady—a very disagreeable woman, by the way—told me that you bought a house on Oak Way but that you were living in this—" He shuddered. "—den of iniquity. Do you intend to spend all your days fornicating now that you're retired?"

"Of *course* not." Iaian grinned. "I intend to spend all my *nights* fornicatin', too. Right now, though, I need a nap. Fornicating's tiring."

"I wouldn't know," Grovis said. "I need to speak with you."

"It's nice t'need things." Iaian pushed past Grovis and opened the door.

To his annoyance, his former partner followed him. "There's something very wrong going on at the castle, and I'm not sure what to do about it."

Iaian rolled his eyes as he slowly walked upstairs. "You're the one with the shiny new purple cloak, boy, *you* figure it out." His knees cracked and he started to question the efficacy of choosing a residence that required stairs to access in which to spend his declining years. "It's funny, I always figured it'd be a great day for the Guard when Osric finally quit or died or retired or whatever. Shoulda known they'd find the one shitbrain who's worse."

Iaian went into his apartment, and wanted to slam the door in Grovis's face, but the younger man moved too quickly and dashed inside, his purple cloak billowing behind him. Iaian was barely able to avoid closing the door on the cloak, which would, he thought, have been poetic justice, but sadly would have done little to get rid of him any faster.

"I'm serious, Iaian, I'm in a bit of a pickle and I need your advice."

Iaian went over to the basin to rinse his hands. "I'm serious, too. You're the captain an' I'm retired. I don't see what the hell you need me for." He gave Grovis a dirty look as he dried his hands with a cloth towel. " 'Sides, I don't recall you thinkin' much'a my opinion back when we were partners."

"It was barely a week ago that we were partners, Iaian. And I don't know what to do about this problem, and it relates to ongoing investigations, so I can't talk to the other detectives about it—in fact, it's what I tell them that's the problem. You have the advantage of being someone who understands the squadroom but who is no longer in it. I need that perspective."

Much as he hated to admit it, Grovis was actually making logical sense.

And then he put the capper on it: "Besides, you're my partner. Ghandurha knows you spent enough time drilling it into me that partners look out for each other. Well, dammit, I need someone to look out for me."

I taught the little shit too well. "All right, fine, tell me what the damn problem is." Iaian sat down on the large easy chair, one of only two pieces of furniture he brought from the place he'd shared with his wife. The other was the day bed that he'd been sleeping on for almost two decades.

Grovis looked around trying to find a place to sit, then realized there was none beyond what Iaian was seated on

"I don't plan to be entertainin' much," he said by way of explanation. "Get on with it and get outta here so I can take my damn nap."

"Very well." Grovis took a deep breath, and proceeded to tell Iaian about Lord Blayk's sweeping changes, not only to the Castle Guard, but to Cliff's End in general, with particular note of Torin's comments about a war footing. He went on to mention the lord's revelation that he didn't think they should be looking into Lord Albin's death at all, and finished with Dru and Aleta's information from Gobink about their employer being a gnome with a lisp who came from Iaron.

"Okay," Iaian said, not sure where he was going with all this.

"Lord Blayk has a secretary who follows him everywhere and keeps track of everything for him. He brought him back from Iaron with him. He's a gnome with a lisp."

"Iaron's a pretty big city-state." Iaian shrugged. "There's bound t'be more'n one lisping gnome there."

"But what if it *is* the lord's aide? That makes Lord Blayk complicit in the attempt on King Marcus and Queen Marta! Worse, what if he's also responsible for poisoning Lord Albin?"

Iaian couldn't believe he was hearing this. "Why is any'a this even a question?"

"I beg your pardon?"

"Look, even before Albin made the Castle Guard into a police force, the mandate was t'enforce the lord and lady's laws, right?"

"Yes, of course."

"Well, Lord Blayk's the first half'a that now. He's the law. Hell, he's the guy who controls the money."

"Yes, but—"

Iaian held up a hand. "There ain't no 'but' here. Yeah, it *might* be that he plotted to kill Daddy and the king and queen. It also *might* be that some other lisping gnome's got regicidal tendencies an' the rest of it's just Blayk puttin' his mark on Cliff's End. Hell, Albin did the same thing when he took over."

"Yes, but—"

"You ain't listenin'!" Iaian stood up. "Look at it this way, boy. Whaddaya get if you investigate Blayk?"

"I—"

"Either he *is* behind all this like you think he might, in which case it don't matter, 'cause he's the boss and he'll shitcan anything you do. Or he *ain't* behind it, in which case you falsely accused the leader'a the largest, most prosperous city-state in Flingaria of the worst crime on the books. And in both cases, the end result's gonna be the same: he'll toss you an' any detectives you drag into it out on your asses. Now that's fine for you, 'cause you got Daddy's money to cushion the blow. But what do Torin and Dru and Aleta and the rest of 'em do? Huh?"

Grovis was staring intently at the floor. "But the law states—"

"Oh, for Wiate's sake, boy, ain't you learned a damn thing? It don't matter for shit what the law states. What matters is what the people in power *say* matters. If that means they kiss off the law, that's what it means. Only people who can do what you wanna do is the king an' queen, so 'less you plan on travelin' to Velessa t'give 'em your evidence—which barely exists right now—you're shit outta luck."

Grovis was still staring at the floor.

"Anythin' else? Maybe you want me t'remind you how to take a piss?"

"No! No, thank you, I'll—I'll see myself out."

Slump-shouldered, Grovis turned to leave the apartment. For which Iaian was grateful, because he needed the nap more than ever now.

Tonight, I'll just stick with that one blonde . . .

FOURTEEN

Manfred was disheartened at how quiet it was in the Old Ball and Chain when he entered.

The place was as crowded as ever, and there was still plenty of noise, but the post-day-shift gathering was usually so loud you could only hear a conversation if it was right near your ear. Not so much, tonight. Or, indeed, any night since the double whammy of Lieutenant Hawk's death and Lord Albin's.

He had been hoping that the funeral would break the trend, but with everything that had happened since . . .

Jared's voice at one of the tables carried to where he was standing—more evidence, as normally he'd only hear even Jared's booming voice if he was right on top of him at the Chain at this hour. "I can't believe those shit-suckers're makin' you ride a desk!"

Following the voice, he saw Jared, along with several other guards from Dragon, including Simon, Ebnig, Salvit, and a dwarf he didn't recognize sitting at one of the tables in the rear. Glancing further back, Manfred saw that Torin, Danthres, Aleta, Dru, and Kellan were all seated at the corner table where the detectives usually sat. Manfred had been looking forward to being allowed to sit at that table for months, but now that he could, he found himself wanting to sit with Jared and the others.

However, leaving aside anything else, he had news for Torin—and eventually for Grovis, of course, but he wanted to tell his new partner first, especially since it was mostly a complete lack of news.

"Hey, Manfred!" Jared cried out. "C'mon over here a sec an' meetcher replacement."

Manfred came over and stood between Jared and Simon. "How you guys doing?"

"Shitty," Simon said before anyone else could answer. "I failed my damn sword qualification, can you believe that shit? They got me on a desk for two weeks before I can try again."

Frowning, Manfred said, "The quals ain't till midwinter."

"Tell that t'Lord Blayk," Jared said bitterly. "He's makin' all of us test, an' we ride a desk if we don't pass."

"That's insane."

"You aren't wrong, you're not." The dwarf who said that held out a hand. "I'm Zinnig—they transferred me over from Mermaid, they did."

Manfred returned the handshake. "Glad to meet you."

Zinnig turned to Jared. "Oh, hey, is this the one?"

"Huh?" Jared scowled, then brightened. "Oh, yeah! We still ain't found Beffel yet, but you said you was askin' for info on 'im, right?"

Manfred nodded.

"I know him from the docks, I do," Zinnig said. "He lives in the Swamp, but spends all his days on the docks running errands for the ships. Carries messages, fetches people, that sorta thing, he does."

"Who's he been working for lately?" Manfred asked.

"That's the funny thing—he usually works for lots of folks, he does, but lately it's been all for the *Esmerelda*. Like he went exclusive with them, he did."

They chatted for a few more minutes, and Manfred promised to raise a toast to Simon's tragic new career as a desk jockey before finally heading over to the detectives' table. For one thing, he had something good to tell Torin, as that tidbit from Zinnig was the most useful thing he'd found out all day.

Torin was speaking as Manfred worked his way back to the corner table. ". . . and I find myself wondering what Lord Blayk knows about the state of Flingarian politics that we don't." He was drinking an ale, as was almost everyone. A pitcher sat in the center of the table, and Manfred noticed two empty flagons.

"I can't imagine what it might be," Aleta said in reply. She was the only one not drinking an ale, instead partaking of a red wine. "Who would we be fighting against anyhow? There've been no issues with the dwarves, and my people are a disaster. There isn't any kind of naval buildup to go with this, so it can't be one of the island nations."

"Maybe we're takin' on the barbarians up north," Dru said with a snort.

Kellan finally noticed that there was a new arrival. "Manfred, hey! Now we got the whole squad!" He poured some ale into one of the two remaining flagons.

Dru held up his flagon. "Yup. And that means I can finally say this: a toast to Hawk from the *whole* detective squad!"

Cries of "To Hawk" and "For Hawk" and such came from many around the table. Manfred, for his part, took the flagon from Kellan and then banged it against as many of the others' as he could before gulping some down.

He sat between Kellan and Dru. To his disappointment, but lack of surprise, Danthres wasn't making any kind of eye contact with him. He really didn't understand what went wrong there. It had been a magickal night, but after that, she treated him with nothing but disdain—even beyond the usual disdain she displayed toward anyone who wasn't Torin.

Speaking of Torin, he, at least, was willing to make eye contact. "Were you at all successful today, Manfred?"

"Not with the magick shops, no. Most of the shop owners either laughed when I asked about a Keefda stone, or they tried *way* too hard to convince me that they could get one for me cheap."

Torin snorted. "Boneen said they go for five thousand gold."

Manfred nodded. "Right. It might be that one of the ones who said they couldn't get one were lying—or they might've been telling the truth because they already sold it and didn't want to give their client up."

Dru spoke up. "We actually gotta be talkin' to some'a the shops t'see who mighta bought the Snavli charm that hid the weapons from the king and queen's magick detectors. You want, we can ask about the Keefda stone, too."

Frowning, Kellan asked, "What difference would that make? Manfred already asked."

Danthres rolled her eyes. "Use what passes for your brain, Kellan. Manfred's asking about a bar brawl. Nobody's going to give enough of a shit about that to cooperate, because there isn't anything in it for them. But these two are looking into an assassination attempt on the king and queen. Anybody involved in that is risking being boiled in oil. They'll cooperate."

"Is that really ethical?" Aleta was looking at Dru.

"It gets the job done." Dru shrugged. " 'Sides, we gotta look out for each other. 'Specially now, with fish-face in charge."

"Oh," Manfred said after sipping more ale, "something else—I just talked to one of the guards in Dragon who transferred over from Mermaid. Says he knows Beffel—he runs errands for boats all the time, but lately he's been working entirely for the *Esmerelda*. Maybe tomorrow we can check the boat out and . . ."

He trailed off because he noticed that Dru and Aleta were exchanging surprised expressions.

Then Aleta stared intently at Manfred. "The *Esmerelda*? You sure?"

"Hardly surprising," Danthres said dismissively, "Zaile and his crew always have their hands in something. Or several somethings."

Dru was shaking his head. "Yeah, but the *Esmerelda*'s the boat that the assassins came in on."

"What?!" That was Danthres and Torin both, and Manfred couldn't help but sputter his ale at the two of them speaking in unison.

Now it was Torin shaking his head. "This is starting to make an odd kind of sense."

"What is?" Manfred asked.

"Why a five-thousand-gold stone is being used to hide an assault, and also why Beffel has been so reluctant to talk *and* so hard to find. If Gobink's fellow conspirators beat up Beffel in order to make sure he didn't talk to us about them, they wouldn't want Boneen to be able to pick them out of a peel-back."

With a snort, Danthres added, "Of course, it hardly matters now that we don't *have* Boneen . . ."

"Yes, well, perhaps your conversation with Lady Meerka will bear fruit in that regard." Torin turned to Aleta. "You two should definitely canvass the magick shops tomorrow—look for both the charm used by the assassins *and* the Keefda stone."

"Shouldn't we bring this to the captain first?" Aleta asked.

Dru, Danthres, and Torin all snickered. Torin said, "There would be little point."

Putting a hand on his partner's shoulder, Dru said, "Osric is 'the captain.' Grovis is just a shitbrain that got promoted. We can talk to his stupid ass when we actually arrest someone."

"Besides," Danthres said, "it isn't as if that idiot's actually running anything. It's become increasingly obvious that Grovis is simply serving as a conduit for Lord Blayk." She shook her head. "I honestly don't know what's worse, Grovis thinking for himself or Grovis unquestioningly doing whatever the lord says. Whenever Osric disagreed with Lord Albin or one of the other noble shitbrains, he always stood up for us. I can't see Grovis standing up for much of anything."

Manfred was still thinking about the next day's plan. "What if the assassins had both the charm and the stone all along? Or got them wherever they came in from on the *Esmerelda*?"

"Then we're screwed," Danthres said bluntly. She gulped down some ale. "And furthermore—" She interrupted herself with a belch.

Aleta winced. "Must you do that?"

Danthres scowled at Aleta. "Except for you, Shranlaseth, everyone at this table has belched at least once."

"I haven't," Manfred said, raising a hand.

"Everyone who's been here more than a few minutes," Danthres added with a glower at Manfred. *Oh, well, at least I got her to look at me.*

"My name is Aleta—I'm not Shranlaseth anymore, no one is—and I'll thank you to use my name, halfbreed."

"You first."

"Enough, both of you," Torin said.

But Aleta stood up. "Excuse me. The air in here has gotten foul."

She pushed past the various tables to leave the Chain.

Manfred watched her leave, then also got up. "I'm gonna make sure she's okay."

"I'd stay out of her way," Dru said, holding up a cautionary hand.

"We've been serving together in Dragon." Manfred smiled. "I'll be fine, I've learned when to duck while talking to her."

He heard Danthres mutter that it was a waste of time as he left the tavern.

Once he reached the door, he saw Aleta standing in the middle of Meerka Way, fists clenched.

Deliberately approaching her from the left side—nobody approached Aleta from behind, at least not twice—Manfred asked, "You okay?"

"No." She shook her head. "Where does that halfbreed bitch get off talking to me that way?"

"Uhm, I don't know if you've noticed, but she talks like that to *everyone*. Well, except Torin, and even then sometimes."

"No, it's different with me." Aleta sighed. "She treats me like I'm some kind of foul creature."

"Like I said, she's like that with most people. It's her way. And I don't think you're asking the right question."

Now, finally, Aleta looked at him. "What do you mean?"

"Where do *you* get off talking to *her* that way?"

"I beg your pardon?"

Manfred was getting nervous now, as Aleta packed a great deal of menace in those four words, but he soldiered on. "I've watched you, Aleta. You talk to everyone with politeness and respect. And if they outrank you, it's out-and-out deferential, even if you don't respect the person. But not Danthres—her, you treat like something you stepped in, and I've never seen you talk like that to anyone who wasn't a dockrat or a beggar in Goblin. Even that nobleman from Barlin who tried to get you fired after that thing at the theatre, you still called him 'sir.'"

Aleta actually smiled at that. "To his face, of course I did. He had the ear of the lord and lady, he deserved respect."

"And Danthres doesn't?"

"She's a halfbreed!" Aleta said those words as if they explained everything.

And perhaps they did. "So you lied back there."

"I beg your pardon?"

Manfred swallowed. The second utterance of that phrase was even scarier than the first. "You told Danthres you weren't Shranlaseth anymore. Well, you coulda fooled me. You're in the Guard now, and we don't give a shit who your father had sex with."

With that, he took his life into his hands by turning his back on her and walking back into the Chain. He wanted to rejoin his comrades and friends.

FIFTEEN

Dru and Aleta had spent the entire day since roll call going to every magick shop in Cliff's End. They started in Dragon, in part due to the proximity (there were no shops in Unicorn, as that region was entirely residential), but mainly because the more expensive items they were after were more likely to be sold in the shops in Dragon than the ones in Goblin or Mermaid.

Unfortunately, while every owner was, as predicted, completely cooperative once they mentioned they were investigating the attempt on the lives of the king and queen, they weren't actually helpful. Nobody had a Keefda stone—though most would have gratefully sold one if they had one—and only two Snavli charms had been sold in the past year. One was to an elderly man who died at midsummer—according to his widow, he erroneously thought the disease he eventually died of was caused by magick, and that the charm would save him—and the other to a merchant who was passing through Cliff's End and booked passage on a boat to take him south.

Both those Snavli charms were sold in Dragon. They had no luck at the Goblin magick shops—they specialized in cheaper charms and love potions and the like—and when the detectives reached the River Walk that brought them into Mermaid, Dru turned to Aleta. "I think we're pretty much done here."

"There are three magick shops on the River Walk. We've checked every other shop, might as well check them."

Dru sighed. "I guess, but it's all weather charms an' anti-nausea potions in those places."

The time chimes then rang once, indicating that it was half past eighteen. Aleta glanced at Dru. "We've only got half an hour, anyhow, we might as well hit these last three shops, then we can call it a night without having to go back to the castle."

Dru shot her a look. "Why don't you wanna go back to the castle?"

Aleta looked away. "I just don't."

"Look, you gotta deal with Danthres some time. And I'd honestly rather it was sooner than later, 'cause I ain't about to get inna middle'a you two pissin' at each other. As a start, maybe stop callin' her 'half-breed.' She *really* don't like that."

"But it's what she *is*!" Aleta threw up her hands in frustration. "You don't understand."

"Yeah, you're right, I don't. I'm assumin' it's that whole elven purity shit. I get a lotta that from elves when they first show up here. Reality'a life makes 'em get over it right quick, though."

"One of the things they drilled into us in our training with the Shranlaseth was that the most horrible thing an elf can do is to breed with another race. We were trained to kill any halfbreed on sight."

Dru snorted. "Yeah, I wouldn't try that with Danthres."

"Of course, I won't, but—" She let out a long breath, and Dru noticed that her gloved fists were clenched. "It's a lot to overcome."

"Well, then overcome it. C'mon, I've seen how you handle your-self—and I heard Mannit tell the story about the Troll Riots over lunch yesterday, remember? You can do *that*, you can get past your trainin' and see Danthres for what she is."

"And what's that?"

"The biggest pain in the ass you ever met in your life, an' also one'a the best detectives you'll ever work with. When Hawk and me first got promoted, she treated us like shit, about like usual, y'know? But we'd worked with her onna street before, so we kinda expected it. Anyhow, there was this one case, a murder me an' Hawk caught. Turned out that the guy was connected to a series of robberies that Danthres an' Torin were lookin' into. So the four of us worked together, an' I gotta tell ya, I learned more about the job from two days workin' alongside her an' Torin than I did in the year before that as a detective. She's *good*, an' the Guard wouldn't be what it is right now if it wasn't for her."

"And Torin," she added insistently.

Dru rolled his eyes. "Yeah, an' Torin, but Torin only got the job 'cause Osric figured he was the only one could keep her ass in check. He was right, too." He sighed. "I seriously miss Osric. He yelled at me ten times a week whether I needed it or not, but he was a real good boss."

Aleta nodded. "Manfred said something similar about the half—" She cleared her throat. "About Lieutenant Tresyllione last night. I will endeavor to work with her."

"Good."

They approached the entrance to Shrenthorshi's Magick Shop.

Looking up at the sign, Dru smiled, noticing that the name of the store was in both Common and Ra-Telvish. "So I'm gonna go out on a limb an' say that an elf owns this place."

Aleta smirked. "Brilliant detective work, Lieutenant Dru."

"Thank you, Lieutenant lothLathna." Dru bowed, and they both went in.

Sure enough, there was a male elf behind the counter, which was circular, located in the center of the space. He had very short dirty blond hair, and prominent tapered ears, as well as a silk shirt and purple tights. Dru thought he was trying a little too hard, considering he mostly sold to dockrats and tourists.

He was talking to an elderly halfling couple, who were examining potions. "Now, I know everyone says that the Mazur potion is better because it's more expensive and tastes like honey, but I think you'll find that the Wardwood potion is far, far stronger. Mind you, it tastes horrible, but it's also only thirty coppers, as opposed to two silver for the Mazur. Just wash it down with some wine to get rid of the taste, and it'll last half again as long."

The couple exchanged a nod, and then paid the elf the thirty coppers for the Wardwood potion.

As soon as they left, Dru said, "I'm impressed. Most merchants would take the extra twenty coppers an' sold the Mazur."

The elf shrugged. "The Wardwood really is stronger and cheaper, and giving customers good advice is the best way to get them to come back."

Aleta chuckled. "Those two are from Treemark and are here on vacation. They're also very old. You'll be lucky if you ever see them again."

"Perhaps." The elf shrugged. "The principle is a sound one either way. What may I help you officers with?"

"I'm Lieutenant Dru, this is Lieutenant lothLathna."

"A pleasure. I'm Shrenthorshi lothHethra. Are you two here on business or do you wish to make a purchase?"

"Business," Dru said. "We're lookin' into four people who tried to kill the king an' queen at Lord Albin's funeral."

Shrenthorshi's mouth formed an O. "My word. I had no idea anyone tried to do that."

"We got 'em before they could try anything. Well, we got one of 'em—tryin'a find th'other three. Were hopin' you could help us."

"I can't imagine how." Shrenthorshi was sounding a little nervous now, but Dru couldn't tell if that was because of the revelation that someone tried to kill the king and queen or something else. Certainly, everyone they had talked to had been apprehensive at the very notion of the assassination attempt.

Aleta said, "The conspirators bought two really expensive magickal items. A Keefda stone and a Snavli charm."

"Well, believe me, Lieutenants, if I sold a Keefda, I'd be able to retire, and as for a Snavli, I've still got the same three in stock that I had when I opened the store. If there's nothing else?"

Dru no longer had any doubts. Shrenthorshi was very nervous about something. "There's a whole helluva lot else."

Aleta moved forward to lean on the countertop. "You do understand what we're investigating here, yes? The attempted murder of King Marcus and Queen Marta. This isn't something we can simply overlook."

"Look, I—" Suddenly, Shrenthorshi caught sight of something, because his eyes went very wide.

After a moment, Dru realized that he was staring right at the Shranlaseth tattoo that was on Aleta's neck. Only part of it was visible jutting out from the neckline of her armor, but it was a very distinctive Ra-Telvish character.

"You—you—you're Shranla— I can't even say it." Shrenthorshi started to back away from the edge of the counter, only to bump into the other side of it and jump. "Ahh! Look, I know what you people do!"

"And what is that?" Aleta asked sweetly.

"Back home, you lot used to rip people's fingernails out and I don't want my fingernails ripped out!"

"There's an easy way to avoid that." Aleta spoke in a matter-of-fact tone. "Tell us the truth. The actual truth, not the lies you spun a few moments ago."

Dru was leaning casually on the counter. "You think we came in here by accident? We been onto you for a while."

Shrenthorshi put his head in his hands. "Of course you have been, I'm *such* a fool, but the money was just—" He looked up, and Dru saw tears trickling down his cheeks. "Look, I'm sorry, I had no idea it involved anything with the king and queen, he just came in here and offered ten thousand gold for the two items." He shook his head. "I'd only just gotten the Keefda, sold to me by a fellow from Iaron who sold it to pay for his retirement trip to Saptor. And then that fellow came in and asked for it and the Snavli and offered ten thousand . . ."

"Thought you said you could retire on that," Dru said.

"Well, see—" The head went back in the hands. "Oh hell, this is such a nightmare. I had debts, you know? I had taken out a loan to buy this place, and I had some old investments that had gone bad, and I had to pay to remodel this place so it would pass the Brotherhood's annual inspection, and I still owe the contractors for that, and . . ." He broke down and started crying into his palms.

Aleta gave Dru a look that seemed to say, *That person is pathetic!* For his part, Dru just said, "So the buyer paid off all your debts?"

Shrenthorshi nodded into his hands. "I'm finally clear for the first time since I came to Cliff's End. I thought it was the best day of my life, and now I'm going to be boiled in oil."

Slowly, Aleta said, "Well, you may be able to escape that particular fate, but you'll have to cooperate with us."

"Really?" The elf's head popped up from behind his hands. Tears were now streaming down his face. "I'll do anything!"

"A good start," Dru said, "would be the name of the buyer."

"I don't know what that is, I'm sorry. He never told me."

"Course he didn't." Dru sighed. It was never that easy.

"But I can tell you one thing—he was a gnome. And he had a lisp!"

SIXTEEN

ARON FANKELL COULDN'T BELIEVE THAT IT HAD ALL GONE SO COMPLETELY TO SHIT.

Life had been so much simpler during the war. He joined up as a teenager, having just impregnated a girl, and was scared to death of the responsibility. His eagerness to fight for King Marcus and Queen Marta against the Elf Queen was matched only by his eagerness to get away from Yvenna and their child. Besides, the Elf Queen was evil—everyone said she was. Even her own cousin, the famous wizard Olthar lothSirhans, betrayed her because she was so evil. So he served in the army, fighting for the 17th legion under a really good general whose name he couldn't remember—though Fankell did recall that he lost his eye at the end of the war.

The general's eye wasn't the only thing lost when the war ended, either. Fankell utterly lost his direction. Here he was, a young adult whose only skill was in being a soldier. To add some insult to that particular injury, he had no pension, even though he was promised one if he survived. So he spent the next decade taking whatever work he could. After all, he had a child to support. Yvenna died giving birth to their daughter, and Yvenna's parents were very insistent that he pay for at least half of the girl's upbringing.

The problem was, there wasn't a lot of work to be had, as Fankell was far from the only copper-less soldier to be wandering around Flingaria desperate for work. He wound up taking body guarding work for some criminals in Velessa, which went well for a while until they asked him to kill someone. Which Fankell did—he killed plenty during the war, and all anybody gave him were congratulations.

But killing when there wasn't a war on tended to get people's noses out of joint, which rather surprised Fankell. He moved to Treemark, one step ahead of the authorities, and looked for more work.

He wound up doing the same sort of thing in Treemark, only this time it took him a lot longer to get caught.

Unfortunately, he then had a bigger problem: he couldn't earn money in a dungeon. Yvenna's parents were elderly, and little Yvenna (they named her after her late mother, which just confused Fankell) was sickly, so they needed the money Fankell sent to them every month. Because Treemark only executed criminals who committed capital crimes once a year at midwinter—supposedly it was to build up the tourist trade, which was pretty moribund at that time of year—and Fankell had been caught in the spring, he was going to have a long wait in the dungeon.

Then Gobink showed up. One of the black-market magick dealers he worked for hired the *Esmerelda* to move merchandise, and he'd first met Gobink then. The dwarf had heard about Fankell being imprisoned, and said he wanted to help. He promised to bribe the Treemark City Guard to free him, and then he'd do a job for Gobink's employer. Said job would be an assassination attempt that, if he was caught, would result in his death. Fankell was under a death sentence already, so he didn't much see the point, nor did he have any great desire to kill the king and queen, considering their war was kind enough to get him away from the pregnant Yvenna. Had he not been able to enlist, he would've been forced into fatherhood, a state at which he had neither skill nor desire to enter.

By the same token, he did feel responsible for little Yvenna, so Gobink sweetened the deal by promising that Yvenna's grandparents would be given a thousand gold.

That convinced Fankell to agree to it. Yvenna would never have to worry about anything after receiving that much coin.

He'd joined Gobink in Crestwood, and then they boarded the *Esmerelda*, along with another dwarf and another human. Fankell couldn't remember their names any more than he remembered the general's. He barely remembered Gobink's. He sometimes wondered if that was why Yvenna's parents named the girl Yvenna, so it would be easier for Fankell to remember it. He also wondered sometimes if he just thought of the girl as Yvenna, and that they'd in fact named her something else and he'd forgotten it so he just thought of her with her mother's name.

They'd had to live a few months in Cliff's End, so they each found places to live in different parts of town. Fankell rented a room in a boarding house on Salmon Alley near the docks. During those months, the only communication he had from Gobink was to buy three vials of a particular type of poison, one that apparently was used as a weed-killer, and to give the dwarf one vial at the Dog and Duck the following morning. It turned out that the shop only had two vials left, as the market for that particular type of poison had lessened since it was discovered that the poison was leading to diseased rabbits.

When Fankell asked what to do with the other vial, Gobink simply said, "Let's hope we don't need that one. Hang onto it for now."

Then came another summons to the Dog and Duck, where they were each given rooms so they could be ready to go at a moment's notice.

Finally, on the day of Lord Albin's funeral, they were each given Thevit daggers and Snavli charms, and instructions on how to proceed. It had all gone very well, at first. They worked their way through the crowd separately but as a unit, and then they waited for Gobink's signal for them to throw their daggers at the monarchs. Fankell was given Queen Marta, as was the other dwarf. Gobink and the other human had King Marcus.

It was all fine until he noticed four guards coming toward them through the throngs. And one of them—one of the two without a cloak—was headed straight for him. He reached for Fankell, who panicked and grabbed the guard's wrist, then bit his hand.

He had no idea *why* he bit the guard's hand. It just seemed like the thing to do. Having sufficiently distracted the guard, he lost himself in the sea of people, heading for the exit, hoping the Snavli charm still worked as they passed through the outskirts of Jayka Park. He went straight to the Dog and Duck, where they were all supposed to meet afterward.

The other human, and the dwarf with the eyepatch, they both showed up.

Gobink didn't. And that was a problem.

They agreed to leave Cliff's End as quick as they could—but cautiously. Fankell waited a couple of days in the apartment on Salmon Alley—which he deliberately hadn't given completely up, mostly because he didn't feel like carrying all his stuff, not to mention that other vial of poison, to the Dog and Duck—before heading to the docks.

He wasn't about to try to book passage on the *Esmerelda*. That was too obvious. He had to assume that Gobink had talked. Not that Gobink *would* talk, but Gobink *might* talk, and why take the chance?

Going to the far end of the dock, he talked to the first mate of a small fishing trawler that would take on a passenger if he paid two gold, which Fankell did happily. The first mate then went toward the trawler to talk to his captain—but he was interrupted by a guard.

Not liking the look of that, Fankell immediately beat a hasty retreat. The guard started chasing him, but Fankell had been chased before, and it was the docks at midday—the place was packed with people. He lost the guard as easily as he did during the funeral in Jayka Park.

But now the Castle Guard knew that he was in the docks. Getting out of the city-state via boat was looking less likely.

So he ran to the old port.

One of the other boarders in the house on Salmon Alley where Fankell had been living was an old sailor named Throndik, who just loved to go on and on about the history of Cliff's End. While he sat in the common room of the boarding house waiting for a summons from Gobink or the lisping gnome he worked for, Fankell would sit and be regaled by endless stories about how the demesne was founded, how it grew from a castle with a port to a city-state, the development of Oak Way as a thoroughfare to separate the rich from the not-so-rich, the establishment of the precincts to demarcate sections, and—most important to Fankell just at the moment—the abandoning of the natural port at the end of Salmon Alley due to overcrowding and the construction of the current docks.

"Why I remember," Throndik said, "hearin' old Cap'n Nat goin' on about how much better things were in the old port. He didn't have no truck with the new port, did Cap'n Nat, he thought things should always be the way they was. I can sorta see his point, but there ain't no room for all the boats we're gettin' nowadays in the old port. Don't nobody go there, neither, what with all the boardwalks an' docks an' things fallin' to pieces. Why I heard tell that that was where Corvin the vampire hunter killed the last vampire b'fore the Brotherhood'a Wizards wiped 'em all out."

After that, Throndik started talking about vampires, which actually was of more interest to Fankell at the time than the history of a city-state he'd never been to before and would—one way or another—never set foot in again after this job was concluded.

But now he was recalling that part of Throndik's nattering with crystal clarity. He needed to be somewhere no one would go to try to find him, so what better place than the old port? As he ran down the aptly named Old Port Way to where it intersected with Salmon Alley, he found an overgrown area where the ground curved into a natural inlet that was pocked with rotted wood docks. Fankell figured he'd have no trouble hiding here.

He slowly worked his way through the docks, hoping like hell that nobody was following him. Reaching for his sash, he felt the Thevit dagger that was holstered there. Worse came to worse, he'd use it. After all, he was set to kill the king and queen with it, so killing a guard was not as big a deal. His death sentence had already been passed in Treemark, and Yvenna was already taken care of, so Fankell had nothing to lose.

Just ahead was a broken-down old port with a huge hole in the center. Fankell liked the look of that. After clambering up onto the deck — the steps onto it were long since shattered — he looked down the hole and saw a nice little cubby that looked as comfortable as a space barely wider than two people surrounded by rotting wood could possibly be, and he slowly lowered himself down into it.

Yes, this is good. No one will ever find me here.

Unsheathing his dagger, he sat looking up at the hole, waiting to see if anyone showed up.

This gave him a goodly amount of time to sit and think. Mostly about how warm it was in this hole. Autumn was approaching, so the weather was fairly mild in Cliff's End, but inside this tiny space, it was hot and humid. Sweat soaked through all of his clothes, and he started to have trouble maintaining his grip on the dagger's handle.

As he stared up at the hole he'd climbed through, he wondered if perhaps he hadn't thought all of this through. For one thing, he could hardly stay in this hole forever. Sooner or later, he'd need food and water. In fact, he was getting to the point now where he needed water rather badly.

But he knew, just *knew,* that if he stuck his head up out of this hole, the entire Castle Guard would see him.

Or maybe not. Maybe the guard couldn't tell where he went. Or maybe they wouldn't come to the old port.

He was really getting very thirsty.

A loud squeak startled him, and he dropped his dagger. Fumbling for it, he saw a massive rat streak across the space, suddenly stopping to stare right at him with red eyes.

Fankell thrust his dagger outward toward the rat. "Get away from me!"

The rat seemed wholly unintimidated, a feeling Fankell most assuredly did not share. He also could swear that the rat's teeth were getting bigger.

The rat then leapt right at him, and Fankell screamed, waving the dagger around and climbing back out of the hole as best he could. At some point, he dropped the dagger again, but he didn't care because the rat was chewing on his shirttail and he just had to get out of there, so he clambered up and struggled to get up onto what was left of the dock—

—only to find himself at the wrong end of a sword. The rat was still chewing away at his shirttail, but he found he couldn't bring himself to move, what with the point of the sword's proximity to his neck.

The sword was being held by an elven woman wearing Guard armor and a brown cloak. Thanks to Throndik, he knew that she had to be one of the detectives that solved big crimes, because of that cloak. He wondered why a detective was after him.

He also wondered when she'd lower the sword. Or if she'd just wait until the rat chewed through to his stomach.

Then she smiled unpleasantly and reached out with her left hand to grab the rat. Its teeth were still lodged in Fankell's shirt, but she squeezed it, and suddenly it wasn't nibbling anymore.

Tossing the now-dead rat into the Garamin Sea to her right, the elf woman called out to her left. "I told you the rats would work."

"Long as I ain't the one touchin' 'em, we're fine."

Fankell heard the voice of what he assumed was another guard. He refused to take his eye off the sword point near his throat.

"I'm Lieutenant lothLathna," the woman said, "and this is my partner Lieutenant Dru. What's your name?"

To that, Fankell said nothing, though he did swallow very hard. He wasn't about to tell the guards anything. If he talked, he put Yvenna in danger. (And Yvenna's grandparents, too, but Fankell didn't really care much if *they* were boiled in oil.)

After Fankell remained quiet for several moments, Dru said, "Can we get outta here, please? I *hate* this place. A vampire almost killed me an' Hawk here a little while back."

At that, lothLathna frowned and looked away. "A *little* while? Vampires were wiped out five years ago."

"One of 'em wasn't. Long story, which I'll gladly tell you all about when we're *not here.*"

Fankell considered and rejected taking advantage of lothLathna's distraction to try to make a run for it. Her casual one-handed murder of a rat was the basis of the rejection.

Instead, he let her and Dru lead him away from the old port and to the castle. Where he intended to maintain his silence. Gobink gave him another chance to live and enough coin to keep his daughter healthy. And talking would be a death sentence for his daughter.

WHEN TORIN SAW THE SUSPECT THAT ALETA AND DRU BROUGHT INTO THE squadroom, he nearly fell over from surprise.

Aleta put him in one of the interview rooms and closed the door. Turning to Jonas, she said, "Sergeant, would you please go locate Micah? I want him to guard the prisoner." At Jonas's questioning look, Aleta added, "That's the one who bit Micah in Jayka Park."

Jonas nodded. "Right away, Lieutenant."

The sergeant departed, his green cloak billowing behind him. Torin remained at his desk, having just finished the last of his attempts to talk to the nobility, none of which had borne fruit, as they either refused to speak, didn't have time to speak, or both. Lord Blayk had the castle hopping, and it was all of the same tenor — Cliff's End was preparing to fight a war. Or at least preparing to be prepared to fight a war.

Manfred was with him in the squadroom. Kellan and Danthres had been summoned to Lady Meerka's office — which surprised everyone, since Danthres had been told to report to her at the end of each shift, and that wouldn't happen for several more hours.

Dru immediately started telling the two of them about how they nabbed their suspect. "You shoulda seen Aleta in action. We got us a message from Mannit, sayin' one'a his guys saw someone that matched one'a the descriptions tryin'a book passage on the *Blind Luck.*"

Manfred snorted. "Really?"

"Yeah, talk about the wrong one t'pick. Anyhow, this guy legs it soon's he realizes he's been made, heads straight for the old port. Most'a the Mermaid guards don't want no part'a that—an' I don't either, t'be honest, not since that shit with Corvin an' the vampire—but Aleta just heads right on in. She finds a buncha rats, and just all casual-like, starts grabbin' 'em an' shovin' 'em into the old broken-down docks. Eventually, this shitbrain sticks his head out, an' we got him."

"That's amazing!" Manfred said.

Aleta shrugged. "That's tactics. People are afraid of rats for some inexplicable reason—they're perfectly safe as long as they don't bite you, but that's true of most animals—so it makes sense to use them to flush people out of hiding."

"I ain't even told the best part yet!" Dru's enthusiasm was entertaining for Torin to watch—and gratifying, too, since he'd been understandably morose since Hawk's death. "So this guy pops outta the hole in the dock, an' the rat's still nibblin' on his shirt! Aleta reaches over, grabs the rat, an' squeezes the thing t'death right in front'a the guy."

Again, Aleta shrugged. "I was hoping it might work as intimidation, but he refuses to speak. It's Gobink all over again."

"Actually, it isn't," Torin said. "That man's name is Aron Fankell. He served with me in the 17th under Osric during the war."

The three detectives all stopped to stare at Torin. For his part, Torin just smiled.

Aleta nodded slowly. "Gobink said one of the assassins was named Aron."

Manfred said, "I saw him stare right at you when he came in. Why didn't he recognize you?"

"I didn't have the beard when we served together, and Fankell never had the best memory in Flingaria."

Dru turned to Aleta. "'Member what Olaf said? Gobink was the only one who'd been in the Dog an' Duck since the *Esmerelda* brought 'em into town a few months back. The other three checked in right after Hawk died."

Aleta nodded. "Which means he was renting rooms somewhere. Now that we have the full name that matches the description, we should look into that."

"Manfred and I can assist." Torin got to his feet. "Beffel still hasn't turned up, and it's already clear that our cases are related."

Dru nodded. "Thanks, Torin." Micah came in just then, accompanied by Jonas; Torin noted that his hand was bandaged. "'Ey, Micah, we got a suspect you might remember—the guy who bit you's in 'ere. Take 'im to the hole."

Micah's jaw set. "My pleasure, Lieutenant." He moved toward the interview room door.

"Why a bandage?" Torin asked.

Jonas let out a very loud sigh. "I was informed this morning that healing potions are no longer in the budget for anything that doesn't impede job performance."

Torin shook his head. That was one way to pay for the reinforcing of the docks and the new armor . . .

"C'mon," Dru said after Micah led Fankell out of the interview room, "let's go find where this shitbrain's been livin'."

Just as the four of them were moving toward the door, Grovis walked in through it, accompanied by Danthres, Kellan—and a very familiar diminutive form.

"Boneen!" Torin cried, a grin forming under his beard. "You're back!"

The wizard chuckled. "Astute as ever, ban Wyvald. Lady Meerka spoke to Gunderson, and I was reinstated as magickal examiner, thus cutting short my rather well-earned vacation."

"Impressive," Torin said. "I wouldn't have expected that to happen so quickly, if at all."

Danthres grinned. "It's all about applying pressure where it will do the most good. The lady mentioned that taxes were being raised on the nobility, and she thought it would be a *dandy* idea to do the same for the Brotherhood's property taxes on all ninety-seven magick shops within the demesne's borders—not to mention revealing the truth about what Myk Dourti did ten years ago."

"Excellent." Torin wasn't surprised that just revealing Dourti's murderous impulses would do the trick, as it *had* been a decade. But nothing annoyed wizards more than affecting their ability to turn a profit.

Grovis said, "Boneen will be performing a peel-back on Lord Albin's sitting room posthaste."

"*Not* posthaste," Boneen said tartly, "when I've recovered enough from two Teleport Spells."

"Two?" Manfred asked.

"One to bring himself," Kellan said, "and the other t'bring his stuff back t'the basement."

"Good." Torin was still grinning. "The basement room being empty was rather disturbing."

"So's your grin, ban Wyvald. Excuse me, I must go make sure everything's in place downstairs and make sure my sprite is still available. I also need a nap. I'll be back in two hours to cast the peel-back."

As Boneen waddled out of the squadroom, Grovis asked, "And where were you all going?"

Aleta filled Grovis in quickly on Fankell, also finally informing Grovis of the connection between their case and the Beffel case—the *Esmerelda*, Shrenthorshi's Magick Shop—as well as another mention of their lisping gnome.

"The lisping gnome bought both magick items?" Grovis asked.

Nodding, Aleta said, "Why, is that important?"

"No, no, no, no, not important at all, simply making sure all bases are covered. By all means, Torin, Manfred, assist Dru and Aleta, since it seems that Beffel is part of the conspiracy to, ah, to kill the king and queen. It seems you were, ah, right after all, Torin."

"Is something wrong, Captain?" Torin asked. Grovis seemed suddenly out of sorts.

"No, no, no, nothing at all." Grovis's nervous tone belied his words, but before Torin could query him further, he retreated to his office. "Carry on, and let me know what you find."

SEVENTEEN

When Grovis was summoned to Lord Blayk's office, he felt the need to stop in the kitchen for a mug of tea. He needed something to settle his stomach.

To Grovis's great relief, the lisping gnome who had come up multiple times in the investigation of the assassination attempt on the king and queen was not present in the office. It was just the lord of the demesne, who was reading over a slate of the type that the gnome was always carrying.

Setting it aside, Blayk stared angrily at Grovis. "Captain, do you recall what my final words were to you when you were last in this office?"

"Well, my lord, you see—"

Blayk, however, was being rhetorical, and interrupted. "They were that if I heard of Lieutenant ban Wyvald asking around the castle about Father's death, there would be trouble."

"Yes, my lord. But you see—"

"This morning, ban Wyvald was asking around the castle about Father's death. Do you not wish to keep your job, *Captain* Grovis?"

"I do wish to keep my job, my lord, yes."

Placing his palms flat on his desk, Blayk tightly asked, "Then why did you allow ban Wyvald to continue to involve himself in an investigation that I assigned to Lieutenants Tresyllione and Kellan, and which should have been over with by now?"

"Because I was unaware that Torin was still involved in that investigation." Which was the truth. In fact, until he arrived in the lord's office, he hadn't been aware that Torin had been making more inquiries. Of course, he hadn't actually informed Torin of Lord Blayk's desire that he remove himself from the inquiry, distracted as he was by the likelihood that Blayk's gnome aide was part of the conspiracy. Grovis's sense of self-preservation kicked in and stopped him from informing Blayk of that particular lapse.

"Have you no control over your subordinates, Grovis?"

Now, though, Grovis felt it was time for a bit of truth. "No, my lord, I do not."

"And why is that?"

"Because, my lord, as I indicated to you when last we spoke, I do not have the respect or loyalty of my subordinates." He allowed himself to smile a bit. "In fact, most of them view *me* as *their* subordinate, as they did the entire time I served as a lieutenant. Captain Osric earned the respect of the squadroom by his history and his actions, but I'm afraid, my lord, that my own history is only that of a poor detective and a wealthy imbecile who was undeservedly brought into the Castle Guard at the rank of lieutenant without moving up the ranks."

Dismissively, Blayk said, "Your breeding makes your going through the ranks redundant, they should understand that. Besides, ban Wyvald also came in at the lieutenant rank."

"An action that, I'm told, caused problems during the early days of his service. However, Torin is a superb detective, and he earned the respect of the others. I, however, never did, and giving me a purple cloak has done nothing to grant it to me. In fact, it may have done more harm than good, as they now view me as little more than your errand boy. Because of that, they do not always inform me of their activities."

"*Make* them, Grovis." Blayk tugged on the ends of his mustache. "I do not appreciate being blindsided. Bad enough that my mother brought that wizard back, but there is little I may do about that."

"In fact, my lord, there is little you *should* do." Grovis put a hand to his forehead, wiping away a prodigious amount of sweat. Only then did he realize just how frightened he was—yet here he was, barging ahead and committing that most egregious of mistakes, speaking truth to power. Iaian's words about not annoying the person who controlled the purse strings rang in his head. "The magickal examiner is a valuable part of the Castle Guard's investigatory function."

"The Castle Guard's 'investigatory function' is a very minor part of its purview, Captain, and it will become less so as time goes on. That little wizard's presence is a waste." He let out a long breath. "That, at least, is not your doing, but my mother's. I will deal with her in my own time, but meanwhile, I want you to take control of your lieutenants. *Anyone* who disobeys my instructions will be removed from their posts, is that understood?"

"Yes, sir, it is."

"Good. How is the investigation into the assassination attempt proceeding?"

Grovis opened his mouth and closed it. He'd already gone against Iaian's advice too much in this conversation. It would not do at all to reveal the numerous references to a lisping gnome, especially since he himself was the only one who knew that Blayk's aide fit that particular description.

Finally, he said, "We have two of the four assassins in custody, and we know both their names. As we speak, Torin, Manfred, Dru, and Aleta are attempting to ascertain where one of the assassins was living in the weeks between his arrival in Cliff's End and the funeral."

Blayk's eyes widened. "You know when they arrived?"

"Yes, my lord, we know when they came in, what ship they came in on, and what at least two of them were paid. We also know that they were aided by a halfling, who was assaulted in order to stay quiet. The halfling in question has gone into hiding, unfortunately." He hesitated. "Sadly, we do not know the name of their employer, and only have the vaguest description of him."

"So even with all your people have found, you are not close to learning who is behind this?"

"Not yet, my lord, but we're hardly through investigating, either. We're still searching for the halfling and the other two assassins."

"All right, then. I have been receiving daily messages from Velessa asking for our progress. Being able to tell tomorrow's messenger that we have two suspects in custody will, I hope, serve to tone down the harassment a bit." Lord Blayk sighed and picked up another slate. "Very well, Captain, you may go. And please make sure my orders are carried out to the letter—or I shall find a captain who will."

"Of course, my lord." Again, Grovis practically ran out of the office, sweat pouring from his forehead.

He returned to the squadroom just as the time chimes rang the end of shift. There was nobody in the squadroom, save for a quickly departing Sergeant Jonas, and Grovis wondered if everyone had simply gone home and not bothered to tell him. This annoyed him, but didn't surprise him. Before Lord Albin died, no one would ever have dreamed of keeping Osric so completely in the dark, but the detectives were routinely doing so with Grovis.

And what was he to do? The only option Lord Blayk had given him was to fire anyone who disobeyed him, but all that would accomplish was to have an empty squadroom inside a week.

Perhaps that's what he wants, Grovis mused, recalling the lord's comment about the investigatory function of the detectives becoming less relevant. He wondered what that even meant for the future of the Guard.

Just as he was about to go into his office to gather his things and go home to give his father yet another evasive answer as to how his day went, he heard a commotion. Turning, he saw all six of his lieutenants, and Boneen, enter the squadroom.

"Ah, Grovis, you're here," Torin, who was the first one in, said. "Good. We have a bit of news."

"Several bits, actually," Danthres added. "Starting with the results of our newly reinstated M.E.'s peel-back."

Grovis swallowed. "What did you find, Boneen?"

"Nothing good, I'm afraid. Lady Meerka's suspicions were correct. A young man entered the sitting room and introduced poison into the mug that Lord Albin used when he drank in that room."

"Oh dear." Grovis didn't like this one bit. Lord Blayk was already unhappy about having to even open this case, and when he learned it was justified, he would go through the roof. Again.

"You're underselling it, Grovis," Danthres said. "Lord Albin was *murdered*. We have to take action immediately."

"Perhaps." Grovis refused to give in to Danthres's paranoia. Or her tiresome insistence on being right all the time. "Were you able to ascertain Fankell's place of residence?"

"Yes," Torin said, "and that's rather an issue. You see, we found among his personal effects a bottle of Emet poison."

Grovis frowned. "I've not heard of that."

Dru rolled his eyes. "Can tell you never had a garden."

"We in fact have a most excellent garden behind our—"

"You ever actually do any work in it?"

That brought Grovis up short. "Of *course* not!"

"Then you never had a garden, you just got a nice buncha plants to look at near your house. Emet poison's what we used t'use on weeds before they found out that rabbits were eatin' it and gettin' all diseased. Can't hardly find it anymore."

Grovis was now completely confused. "Then how did Lord Albin's murderer get his hands on it?"

Torin then held up a vial that was decorated with a flower logo. "I suspect that it was from the same merchant where Fankell procured his vial of the same stuff."

Now Grovis's eyes goggled. "Wait, *Fankell* had the poison? Are you saying that he also killed Lord Albin?"

"No," Boneen said, to Grovis's relief. "The person I saw in the peel-back did not look at all like the person currently in your dungeon."

Dru asked, "Hey, Boneen, can you show us what the guy looked like?"

Reaching into a pouch, Boneen said, "I took the liberty of creating a crystal." He took one out and it projected the image of a rather sour-faced human.

"Holy shit." That was Kellan. "That's Del Francit!"

Danthres whirled upon him. "The pageboy Sir Palrik mentioned?"

Kellan nodded. "But he's dead. He died two weeks ago."

Boneen frowned. "The poison was applied two weeks ago. Its effects are slow, and mimic that of Lord Albin's usual late-summer illness. No doubt that contributed to why that particular poison was chosen."

"This Francit was killed in a bar brawl, you said?" Danthres asked.

Kellan nodded. "Lieutenant Iaian caught the case."

It was Grovis's turn to frown. "Wait, that brawl in the Ogre's Breath?"

Again, Kellan nodded.

"We never solved that. Nobody saw who killed him, and the peel-back was inconclusive thanks to some manner of glamour, as I recall."

Boneen squinted. "I recall that, yes. The glamour was very sophisticated, but we assumed that it was because the perpetrators wished to keep themselves from being seen by my peel-back."

Grovis nodded. "We made several inquiries, but while Francit was a generally unpleasant sort, nobody hated him enough to kill him. Well, there was his father, who threw him out after he was fired from the castle, but he had an alibi. We had very little evidence to go on, so when the Elko case came up, Osric put us on it." He shook his head. "So you're saying that there's a connection between one of the people who tried to kill the king and queen and the murder of Lord Albin?"

"The vial used by this Francit person," Boneen said, "is the same style as that ban Wyvald and the others found in Fankell's place of residence."

Aleta added, "We also found a sheath that matches that of the Thevit dagger that Fankell had when we captured him—which, in turn, matches my own recollection of the blades used during the funeral in Jayka Park."

"It's maddening." Danthres shook her head. "We have more and more connections, and it's adding up to quite the web of intrigue. But what we don't have is a single solitary notion of who the ringleader might be. All we have is some lisping gnome."

Grovis winced. There it was again.

"You're the one with the shiny new purple cloak, boy, you figure it out."

"I wanted a man of breeding because aristocrats understand their place in the grand scheme of things, Grovis. Your place is to do as I say."

"And in both cases, the end result's gonna be the same: he'll toss you an' any detectives you drag into it out on your asses. Now that's fine for you, 'cause you got Daddy's money to cushion the blow. But what do Torin and Dru and Aleta and the rest of 'em do? Huh?"

"I want you to take control of your lieutenants. Anyone who disobeys my instructions will be removed from their posts, is that understood?"

"Yeth, thir, abtholutely."

It wasn't just a failed attempt on the king and queen anymore. It was the actual murder of the person who ran the city-state, who was responsible for making the Castle Guard what it was today. And it looked like whoever was responsible for that murder also tried to commit regicide.

Grovis saw no way to come out of this well. His detectives were well on their way to finding out the truth, and if they did so without his help, his hands would be clean with Lord Blayk—but what good would that do him in the long run if the truth was as horrible as it seemed to be? Did he wish to remain on the good side of such a conspirator?

Plus, what if it wasn't Blayk? Iaian had been right, he had no solid proof—right now, they only knew that the two crimes were linked. And even that was tenuous.

Is this what you meant, Daddy, when you said you wished for me to join the Guard to make a man of me? That you wished me to be forced to make such awful decisions with consequences that could affect, not just life or death, but the course of Flingarian history?

Finally, he came to a decision.

"I may be able to help with your lisping gnome."

EIGHTEEN

Blayk stared at the slates that Teffeth had left for him, as well as the scrolls he'd provided. The gnome had, at least, been apologetic about giving him so many things to read. Blayk had asked, "Can you at least prioritize them?"

Teffeth had raised a bushy white eyebrow. "I'm afraid, thir, that thethe *are* the priotithed oneth."

"I was afraid you would say that. No one warned me about this, Teffeth."

"About what, thir?"

"The paperwork. Ruling Cliff's End has been my birthright, and I have been eagerly training for the day when I would do so practically since I was a teenager." He had shaken his head. "All the lessons in politics and diplomacy, all the historical studies, all the tactical training, and no one ever bothered to inform me of the sheer volume of paperwork."

"I'm sure they wanted it to be a thurprithe, thir."

Blayk had sighed. Teffeth was invaluable in so many ways, but his inability to remember protocol was maddening. "I keep telling you, Teffeth, I am now properly referred to as 'my lord.' It is well past time you got used to it." Luckily, Teffeth was so good at the rest of his job, that Blayk generally overlooked it, with only occasional, futile reminders such as this.

"Of courth, thir. Is there anything elthe, thir?"

Another sigh. "No, Teffeth, that will be all."

That had been an hour ago, and Blayk's eyes were starting to glaze over from all the various reports and requisitions and manifests. They had merged into a single blur.

He'd been hoping it would be more fun than this.

His secretary—another staff member, like Teffeth, whom he'd brought back from Iaron, a tall elven woman—stepped in and said, "Lieutenants ban Wyvald and Tresyllione to see you, my lord."

Whatever gratitude he felt at his secretary, at least, remembering his title was leavened by annoyance at those two being together. The whole point of the exercise was to split them up.

It was rapidly becoming apparent that he had overestimated Amilar Grovis's suitability for the job. He had assumed that the banker's son would be a compliant subordinate, but it seemed his compliance bled over into spinelessness, making him ineffective.

Still, if nothing else, yelling at the two detectives would prove a nice palliative from the endless streams of paperwork. "Send them in."

The secretary bowed and departed, with the bearded man from Myverin and the ugly half-elf coming in moments later.

Before Blayk could even say anything, ban Wyvald said, "Our apologies, my lord, we both know that you wished us to remain separated, but our cases found themselves dovetailing."

That brought Blayk up short. "Excuse me?"

"May we sit?" ban Wyvald asked.

Distractedly, Blayk indicated the two guest chairs with a gesture. "Which cases are those, Lieutenants?"

"Actually," ban Wyvald said, "all three active cases in the detective squad have turned out to be linked to each other. It started with a halfling named Beffel, who was assaulted in a tavern, but the people who perpetrated the assault used a Keefda stone—a very rare and expensive magickal item, which hid their identities."

Blayk frowned. "So you were unable to identify them."

"No, but the Keefda stone was unusual to say the least. There are only half a dozen in all Flingaria. Purchasing such an item would require someone of great means—not the type of person who would be engaged in a bar brawl."

That would never have occurred to Blayk. He had to admit to being grudgingly impressed. "So were you able to find out who purchased the stone?"

Tresyllione finally spoke. "As it happens, we were. Or, rather, Dru and Aleta were. You see, they were already looking into Snavli charms that the assassins at Jayka Park were using, so they also inquired about the Keefda. Since they were investigating an attempted regicide—a crime that carries with it a punishment of being boiled in oil—they thought they might get more cooperation and less dissembling."

Tugging on the ends of his mustache, Blayk made a grunting noise. That, too, would never have occurred to him.

"And to everyone's surprise," Tresyllione continued, "the same person purchased *both* items from a magick shop in Mermaid. Sadly, we received no name, as the buyer didn't identify himself, and the shop owner provided only a very basic description."

Blayk nodded. "So the people who tried to kill the king and queen were also responsible for this assault on a halfling? That is fascinating, but I believe Lieutenant Tresyllione was performing my mother's useless investigation into my father's natural death."

"It was *not* a natural death. I'm sorry to inform you of this —" Tresyllione didn't, to Blayk's mind, sound especially apologetic despite her words. "—but your father was, in fact, murdered. The house faerie was correct that he was poisoned. The actual act was committed by a bitter ex-pageboy who was fired from the castle—he was murdered right after administering the poison to your father's favorite drinking mug two weeks prior to when Sir Rommett found his body."

"So the murder is solved, then. And without the waste of a trial, too. Excellent work."

"It's not that simple," Tresyllione said, "as the ex-pageboy in question, a young man named Del Francit, didn't have the means to purchase the poison used. He had no means at all, in fact, and was living on the streets. The poison used is also very rare and hard to obtain—it's called Emet, and it used to be used as a weed-killer."

"What do you mean 'used to be'?" Blayk tilted his head in surprise. "I was under the impression that Emet was fairly common."

"Not for some years, my lord," ban Wyvald said gently. "In fact, the last two vials of it to be found in Cliff's End were both purchased by a man named Aron Fankell—one of the two suspects we've brought in on the king and queen's murder attempt. We found one vial in the boarding house where he'd been living—the other was seen by Boneen on his peel-back of your father's office, used by Francit."

"Whoever conspired to have the king and queen killed also killed your father," Tresyllione said. "And whoever is behind that conspiracy is *not* someone of Francit's station. It had to be someone of noble birth."

"Why do you say that, Lieutenant?" Blayk asked angrily.

"Too much money was thrown around—and too much ignorance. Someone who never got his hands dirty or ever paid close attention to the minutiae of gardening, and so didn't know that Emet poison was rare when he or she commissioned Fankell to buy it. Someone who thinks nothing of spending thousands of gold coins on magick designed to cover up the simplest of crimes. Someone who doesn't realize that attempted coverups often do more to reveal the perpetrator of a crime than a lack of one would."

Grinning, ban Wyvald added, "Had it not been for the use of a Keefda stone, Beffel's assault would have barely been noticed, and likely never been solved. Mind you, getting the information on Francit—which was key to the case—was incredibly difficult. You see, many of the nobility in the castle were far too busy preparing for a war."

Blayk blinked. The change in subject was unexpected—as was the subject in question, as ban Wyvald had no business knowing anything about that. "And what makes you say that, Lieutenant?"

"Certainly nothing in the current political landscape suggests it. Flingaria has been at peace since the Elf Queen's death. Yet both the port and the entryways to the city-state via the Forest of Nimvale are being better secured, the portcullis is being repaired, stronger armor is being requisitioned for the Castle Guard, the guardsmen are being recertified half a year in advance, Sir Palrik's largely ceremonial position of military advisor is now occupied by one of the heroes of Flingaria, new swords are being commissioned by the finest swordmaster in the city-state, taxes are being raised, the least able-bodied guards are being encouraged to retire, and so on."

Now Blayk stood. This was intolerable. "How did you learn this information? The nobles were not to speak of it to the likes of you."

"In fact," Tresyllione said, "the nobles were specifically instructed by Lady Meerka—your mother—to cooperate fully with our investigation."

Glowering at the woman, Blayk said tightly, "*Your* investigation, Lieutenant. I am still not clear as to what Lieutenant ban Wyvald here was doing questioning the nobility when I specifically instructed Captain Grovis to remove you from that duty."

Ban Wyvald leaned back in the guest chair. "Really? I'm afraid that I never received that instruction. In any event, my lord, even leaving aside our discussions with the nobility, we would have been able to learn of your attempt to put Cliff's End on a war footing simply by observation of the actions you have taken with regard to the Castle

Guard, the replacement of Sir Palrik, the repair of the portcullis, and the commissions from Molano."

"Plus, guards talk to each other," Tresyllione said. "For example, several from Mermaid have talked about the tighter security restrictions on the port."

"Yes, well, those restrictions are rather necessary." Blayk rose from his seat, wishing to look down at the detectives instead of across at them. "You say, Lieutenant ban Wyvald, that we are at peace, but that is a temporary state. The elves are beginning to reorganize themselves into a government with their Consortium, and the next logical step after that is a new regime that I guarantee will be inhospitable to humans and dwarves alike."

Tresyllione showed a surprising disdain for this statement, given that the mainstream of elven society viewed her as an abomination. "We met a representative of the Consortium a few weeks ago, my lord. They're focused entirely upon useless war tribunals. I can't imagine they'd even be able to build themselves up to be a threat any time soon."

"Then you lack imagination, Lieutenant," Blayk said. "Since the Consortium formed, the population of the elven lands has increased. Before long, they will have enough for a standing army. And when that happens, it is not Velessa that they will target, but rather Cliff's End. We are the most populous, most prosperous, most important city in Flingaria. Most of the trade that Iaron and Barlin and Treemark and Velessa depend upon comes through here."

Nodding, as if understanding, ban Wyvald said, "So you're concerned that the Elven Consortium is preparing a standing army, so you're doing the same with the Castle Guard?"

"I am glad that you understand, ban Wyvald. Now if there is nothing else—"

"But I'm afraid I don't understand the rush."

Blayk blinked. "Excuse me?"

Tresyllione said, "You've been in power for a week and you've got the entire western wing of the castle running around like headless hobgoblins. It's obvious you're trying to turn the Guard into your pet army and phase out the investigatory elements—why else put an idiot like Grovis in charge, split us up, and get rid of Boneen?"

Teeth clenched, Blayk said, "The Castle Guard *is* my 'pet army,' as you so crudely put it, Lieutenant. I may do with them—with you—as I wish."

"Yes, but you seem very much in a hurry to make us over," Tresyllione said. "Torin's question is valid—why such a rush?"

"That is not your concern."

"Quite right," ban Wyvald said, "our apologies, my lord, we're not here to discuss how you choose to rule the city-state, we're here to inform you of the progress of our investigation."

"Which is considerable," Tresyllione added. "We have the names of all four of the Jayka Park assassins and two of them are in custody. It's only a matter of time before we find the other two."

Blayk was about to comment when he noticed ban Wyvald staring at Blayk's desk. "Those are sensitive documents, Lieutenant."

"Actually, it's the items that aren't documents at all that I was staring at. I noticed that your aide uses slates rather than scrolls."

"Oh, he uses scrolls as well, but the slates are useful for ephemeral information that only needs to be conveyed and not necessarily recorded. Chalk is more readily available than ink, particularly in Iaron, and scrolls tend to take up a great deal of space."

Nodding appreciatively, ban Wyvald said, "A very efficient method."

"It is, in fact, Teffeth who first posed the notion of using slates."

"Teffeth is your aide?" Tresyllione asked.

Blayk nodded. "Of course. He is invaluable. I could not run the city-state without him. Indeed, I doubt I would have made it through the past several years without his assistance."

Tresyllione looked at him quizzically. "Interesting that you say that. Because you were without his services for several weeks."

"What are you talking about?"

"Your aide has a very distinctive lisp, my lord. Therefore his presence in the castle prior to your arrival was noted by several of the staff."

"What of it?" Blayk asked archly. "My mother sent for me when Father became ill. I commonly send Teffeth ahead to prepare for my arrival."

"Oh, and Teffeth did arrive ahead of you after Lady Meerka summoned you, also—but that was his second trip to Cliff's End in recent weeks."

"Impressive," ban Wyvald added, "since Iaron is several days away by horse. But then, a person of means could easily purchase a Teleport

Spell—not available to anyone, but the son of the lord of a demesne? Quite affordable."

Blayk did not like the tenor of this conversation at all. He stood behind his desk and leaned forward, palms flat on a part of the surface that wasn't covered in slates and scrolls. "What are you getting at, Lieutenants?"

Tresyllione smiled unpleasantly. "Earlier, we mentioned that we had only a vague description of the person who purchased the magick and hired Gobink, Fankell, and the other two. He was described as a gnome with a lisp—who was from Iaron."

That brought Blayk up short. He stood upright and found himself with nothing to say.

Then he laughed.

He kept laughing for several seconds.

Wiping a tear from his eye, he turned to look at the two detectives whom he had specifically instructed that Grovis separate because they were too good at their jobs. "Well done, Lieutenants. I have to admit, I knew intellectually that the pair of you were skilled at your jobs, but you exceeded even my expectations. I suppose there were ways I could have covered my tracks a bit better. Indeed, the Keefda stone was, in retrospect, such an obvious blunder."

The two lieutenants exchanged a glance. "So," Tresyllione said slowly, "you admit to being behind the conspiracy to kill the king and queen?"

"And," ban Wyvald added, "to killing your father?"

"I admit to putting the events in motion that led to Father's death, yes. It would be disingenuous to deny it at this point. You have many of the pieces already, and it seems obvious that you will have many more given time." He sat back down at his desk. "But you no longer have that time. I am the lord of this demesne and I hereby declare your investigation to cease. Cliff's End is the greatest city in Flingaria, and it will soon take its rightful place as the center of the world. It would have been easier if those four idiots Teffeth hired had done their job properly, but I suppose the more traditional approach will work."

Tresyllione looked upon him as if he was insane. He supposed a halfbreed malcontent like her would misinterpret his vision as insanity. "You intend to conquer Velessa? With what? The Castle Guard are—"

"Mine, to do with as I will. And I have no need to *conquer* Velessa, I simply intend to declare myself the ruler of all the human and dwarven lands in Flingaria. Any who wish to continue to trade via Cliff's End will have to bend their knee to me—including Marcus and Marta. And if they do not, they will be denied that trade and cripple themselves."

"And if they decide to attack, you'll have fortified the city-state," ban Wyvald said, nodding slowly. "Very audacious."

Blayk shook his head. "I begged Father, I pleaded with him. There was no need for him to toady to those idiot monarchs, they were worth a third of him. He controlled the jewel of the world, and he never once took advantage." He sighed. "Ah, well, no matter. You will, as I said, cease your investigation. If you do not, you will be removed from your posts."

Again, ban Wyvald and Tresyllione exchanged glances.

"You may leave now," Blayk said, since they obviously weren't getting the hint.

Tresyllione stood up. "My lord, we cannot simply let this pass. We must arrest you for the murder of your father and the attempted—"

"Oh, don't be tedious, Lieutenant. The pair of you knew the truth before you walked into this room. You are smart enough to have figured out my rather elaborate plan—and bravo for that—but you are also, I should think, both smart enough to know that it would change nothing."

One of ban Wyvald's bushy red eyebrows rose. "You killed the rightful ruler of Cliff's End and tried to do the same to the rightful rulers of the human lands, and you think nothing changes?"

Blayk made a dismissive gesture. "All the greatest leaders of Flingaria have arisen to power by killing a rightful ruler. Queen Marta's own father became monarch by slicing open King Britt's throat. The greatest autarch in dwarven history was Salvalig, but he only became such by hiring an assassin to deal with Autarch Urlanik. Even the Elf Queen, for all her flaws, was the most successful leader of the elven people, and she united the elves by slaying all the petty monarchs who controlled the various fiefdoms in elf country. And I will be spoken of with the same reverence by history, rest assured, Lieutenants, long past when everyone has forgotten about either of you or of my father's ridiculous experiment in turning the Castle Guard into some manner of policing agency. Now then, I am still lord of the demesne by right of birth. You will leave this office and never speak of *any* of this again. If you do, you shall be arrested and hanged, do I make myself clear?"

A voice came from the doorway to the office. "Very clear, Blayk. Very very clear."

To his horror, Blayk looked up to see his mother standing in the doorway.

Behind her was his secretary, looking stricken. "I'm — I'm sorry, my lord, but she came with the three guards and she insisted on standing and listening by the doorway and I didn't know what — what to do, she *is* the lady of the demesne."

Blayk recovered. "And I am the lord of the demesne by right of bi — "

"No, actually," Mother said as she entered the room, hands on hips. "You're lord of the demesne by right of death, specifically Albin's. As you have admitted to being the cause of that death, it makes your birthright suspect."

"Nonsense." Blayk drew himself up straight. He was not about to let Mother ruin everything. "The law of the demesne states that the eldest son shall take over as lord upon the lord's death. There is no proviso for the cause of the lord's death."

"A technicality," Tresyllione said angrily.

"But a correct one," his mother said, and Blayk smiled triumphantly. "It is true that his place as lord is not changed by the method through which he arrived at it."

Tresyllione was insistent. "Conspiracy to commit murder is still a crime."

"Not if I say it is not," Blayk said defiantly.

"Perhaps," ban Wyvald said, "but there are other jurisdictions to consider here." He raised his voice. "Oh, General, would you join us please?"

A tall man with a thick mustache entered the room, then. Blayk closed his eyes and sighed at the sight of his gray armor and green cloak. His secretary had mentioned that there were *three* guards outside, but he hadn't paid attention. Just like he hadn't paid attention to what using a Keefda stone would do. Or how noticeable Teffeth's lisp might be to someone who hadn't been hearing it all day every day for fifteen years.

The general in the Royal Guard stepped forward. Blayk recognized him as the leader of the contingent who had escorted Marcus and Marta to his father's funeral. "Lord Blayk, in the name of King Marcus and Queen Marta, you are hereby bound into the custody of the Royal Guard for the crime of attempted regicide. You will be brought to Velessa to stand trial after which time you and your conspirators will be boiled in oil."

Blayk just stared at the general for several seconds. He shook his head. "This—this cannot be right. No, I forbid this."

"My lord, please do not make this difficult," the general said tightly. "In deference to your station we will not have you imprisoned or shackled, but—"

"Oh, don't be ridiculous, General," Mother said. "The moment you placed him under arrest he lost all claim to his title. His brother Doval is now lord of the demesne, and he's nothing more than a common criminal. Please feel free to bind him and place him in the dungeon until transportation can be arranged back to Velessa."

Blayk frowned and stared at the general. "Wait—how did you get here from Velessa so quickly?"

With a smile, ban Wyvald said, "Boneen was kind enough to use two Teleport Spells, one to go to Velessa, and one to return with the general. Sadly, asking him to send you, the general, and both Gobink and Fankell, not to mention any others we might find, is a bit much. So you'll be travelling by carriage to Velessa to stand trial."

Shaking his head as the general moved to grab Blayk's arm, he said, "I knew I was right to send that damned mage away."

Tresyllione said to the general, "Have one of the guards show you the way to the hole."

"Of course. This way, my lord."

His *dear* mother said to the general, "He isn't properly referred to as 'my lord' anymore! If you must call him something, go back to 'Sir Blayk,' as he's rightfully that by birth regardless. But he is no longer anyone's lord."

For his part, Blayk wouldn't move, even as the general tugged on his biceps. "How could this have happened? I thought of everything."

Tresyllione favored him with a particularly hideous smile. "Well, not *everything*, obviously."

"Your mistake, my lord—" ban Wyvald cast a glance at Lady Meerka. "—excuse me, Sir Blayk, was to underestimate the Castle Guard. The Guard, sir, is bigger than Danthres and me, bigger than Captain Grovis, bigger than Lady Meerka—bigger even than you."

Witheringly, Blayk said, "How witlessly profound."

"I'll tell Osric you said so."

Now the general tugged on Blayk's arm. "This way *please*, Sir Blayk."

As the general brought him down the hall toward one of the guards assigned to the castle, who would no doubt direct him to the dungeon — and what an awful neologism "the hole" was, he'd been hoping to get that changed — the one small comfort he found himself able to dredge up was that Teffeth calling him "sir" would no longer be a problem.

EPILOGUE

Danthres arrived back in the squadroom in a flash of light alongside Torin, and immediately threw up.

Dru was sitting at his desk and smiling. "Welcome back. Was just thinkin' the squadroom smelled too good."

Danthres had a response in mind, but she was too busy retching to make it, though she did manage an obscene gesture.

Aleta walked in from the kitchen with one of Jonas's wife's pastries. "Oh, not again. Isn't there something you can *do* about that? It's been a week of this."

Breathing heavily, Danthres scowled at the elven woman. "I'm sorry your precious senses are offended by my suffering."

"I'm not offended," Aleta said tightly. "I was concerned for *your* well-being."

Danthres didn't believe that for a second, but she wasn't in a position to argue as she heaved again.

Torin came to her rescue. "We've honestly tried everything. Various tea blends, healing potions, even the simple expedient of Danthres not eating when she knew she'd be teleported any of the half a dozen times we've gone back and forth from Velessa the past week. Nothing has worked. A Teleport Spell is cast, she's somewhere else, she vomits."

Danthres had recovered enough to stand upright again. "Every. Single. Time." It had been a week of going back and forth to testify in the trial. After Blayk was arrested, the detectives still had to round up the other two assassins, then the Royal Guard general had to escort all six prisoners back to Velessa. That took two weeks, and then the trial began, supervised by King Marcus and Queen Marta themselves.

Jonas entered from the captain's office, where he'd been alone, since Grovis was nowhere to be found. He was holding an envelope in his hand. "Ah, Danthres, you received a letter from Saptor Isle."

Torin stared at her. "Javian?"

Shrugging, Danthres reached out for the proffered envelope. "I suppose. I don't know anyone else who's living on Saptor right now that I'm aware of." She tore open the envelope to find a piece of parchment written in a very distinctive hand. "Yes, it's Tharri. I'd know that simply awful handwriting anywhere."

Walking to her, Torin peered over her shoulder to see the letter. "I see what you mean."

"Lil always used to joke that Tharri had to become head of the council because if they made him secretary, no one would ever know what the council accomplished."

Torin laughed, and so did Jonas and Dru. Aleta did as well, but that annoyed Danthres.

Before she could pursue the notion, Grovis walked in with the new lord of the demesne. Doval looked a lot like his brother, albeit with thicker hair and no mustache. But he was also tall, long-necked, wiry, and with an even bigger pot-belly than his older brother.

"Ah, Danthres, Torin," Lord Doval said. He liked to be friendly with the detectives, which Danthres found annoying at first, but given the snide tone Blayk always used when he said, "Lieutenant," Danthres was fine with the familiarity over the alternative. "How goes my brother's trial?"

"Over at last," Torin said. "Sir Blayk, Teffeth, Gobink, Fankell, and the other two assassins were all condemned to be boiled in oil. However, in light of the deal Gobink made, and also due to the pleading by Fankell, the king and queen decided to forego extending that sentence to anyone's family."

Danthres chuckled. "Well, if they followed the letter of *that* law, they'd have to kill Lady Meerka, Lord Doval, and the rest of Cliff's End's ruling family, which would no doubt start the very war that Blayk was trying to instigate."

"Splendid!" Doval then frowned. "Well, you know, not *splendid*, exactly. The man *is* my brother, after all, though I must confess to never really liking him all that much. In any case, I'm glad to hear that the whole sordid business is behind us and that the pair of you can get back to doing what you do best, which is defend law and order in this city-state. And it's past time the Castle Guard got back to that. My father's dream was to make the Guard the finest agency for law-enforcement in all Flingaria, and I intend to continue that dream. None of this silly rubbish about becoming ruler of the human lands, no. Cliff's End is enough, I think. Better to let the king and queen handle all the big stuff, eh?" Doval then clapped his hands in the exact same manner that his brother had, which made Danthres a bit apprehensive. "In any event, I must be off. Captain Grovis has some news, which he'll share with you. Cheerio!"

With that, Lord Doval disappeared into the door back to the other wing of the castle.

Manfred and Kellan walked in a moment later. Jerking a thumb behind him, Manfred said, "Lord Doval seemed to be in a hurry."

Grovis gave a half-smile. "He does always seem to be rushing somewhere. Though I suppose he has a great deal of work to do—not only taking over the demesne, but also undoing everything his brother did."

"Well, he's doin' good on that front," Kellan said. "All the guards that failed weapons testin're back onna streets."

"Yeah, but Molano's pissed that she lost all those contracts for new swords. She's been wanting to upgrade our weaponry for *years* now." Manfred then patted his scabbard. "I finally got my new sword, though."

"And," Torin said happily, "Boneen is completely moved back into his basement lair."

"Well, I'm glad you're all here," Grovis said, "because there are a great many announcements to be made. The first is that today is my last day as a member of the Cliff's End Castle Guard."

Danthres's eyes went wide. The first day Grovis set foot in the squadroom in armor, she thought it was a joke. Of course, the first day Torin did likewise, she'd thought that was a joke, as well, but Torin quickly proved himself worthy. Grovis never really managed that trick. That first day, he seemed like a banker's son miscast in the role of detective, and he'd spent the years since living down to that image.

Grovis continued: "My father has asked me to take over management of the day-to-day operations of our three branches." He smiled. "It seems that my going against the direct wishes of the lord of the demesne and providing the evidence that led to the incarceration of a conspiracy to kill the monarchs has satisfied him that the Guard has made a man of me."

While Danthres would be the first to question that assumption, she wasn't about to look a gift unicorn in the mouth. She found herself bursting out with the word, "Congratulations!"

Grovis sounded as surprised at the sentiment as Danthres was at the uttering of it. "Thank you, Danthres, that's very kind. I must say that I view this change in my life with a surprising amount of ambivalence. I've come to truly enjoy my time in the Castle Guard, and I'm not entirely sure I wish to leave." He blew out a breath. "However, I believe we can all agree that I was a terrible captain, and the Guard is far better off *without* my sterling leadership."

Everyone chuckled at that, and Danthres had to admit to being impressed. "Well done, Grovis. I wouldn't have credited you with that level of self-awareness."

"Neither would I," Grovis said conspiratorially. "But then, even the meanest intelligence could see what a poor captain I was."

Again, Danthres surprised herself with her own words. "Grovis, the most important lesson I learned from Osric—because it's something he had to do for me more times than I can count—is that the most important task leaders have is to safeguard and protect the lives of those that they lead. You could very easily have kept what you knew about Teffeth from us."

"I appreciate that, Danthres, but someone would have heard him talk eventually."

"The point is," and Danthres now walked over and put her hands on Grovis's shoulders, "you were mostly a dreadful captain, it's true, but in the end you got it right. And I, at least, appreciate that."

Grovis closed his eyes and smiled gratefully. "Thank you, Danthres."

With that, Danthres moved back to her desk. "So the important question is, who's the new captain?"

That got Grovis to smile. "Lord Doval actually consulted me on the subject of my replacement, which I must say was a welcome change. We both agreed that the best person for the job—"

Danthres steeled herself. She knew it wasn't going to be her—the entire nobility would rebel at the notion, and so honestly would she, as she had no patience for the job—and after her Torin was the seniormost detective. And in truth, she knew he'd make a great captain, and the bump in pay would mean he could finally afford to get a better place to live than the awful apartment he was currently in.

"—is Dru."

Blinking, Danthres looked over at the detective, who was staring wide-eyed at Grovis. "Say *what*?"

"I told Lord Doval, and he agreed, that it would be unwise to break up the partner team of Torin and Danthres, as their remaining together was in the best interests of the continued well being of the city-state. Dru, you're the seniormost detective after them, and I also think that you would do a fine job." He glanced at Danthres. "You already *know* what makes a good captain."

"I—" Dru just stared ahead for a minute. "Shit. I mean, yeah, great! Sure as shit could use the money, an' I think after what happened to Hawk, Zan'll be happy for me to get my ass off the streets."

Aleta said, "If you don't mind my saying so, the feeling I have gotten the past month is that your heart is not truly in being a detective any longer."

Dru nodded slowly. "Yeah." He stood up and offered Grovis his hand. "Anyhow, I'll take the job. No problem."

Aleta began to applaud, and the rest of the squadroom followed suit, though Danthres was slow to do so. Not because she was unhappy for Dru—on the contrary, he was an excellent choice—but because Aleta was the one who started it.

At the very least him getting it meant she got to keep her partner. *And if you'd told my ten-years-younger self that I'd be grateful to be keeping Torin as a partner. . .* She shook her head.

As the applause died down, Grovis said, "However, I don't wish Torin or Danthres to feel as if they've been slighted—or that they aren't appreciated. I suggested also to Lord Doval that we create the position of senior detective, and award those positions to Lieutenants ban Wyvald and Tresyllione."

Now it was Danthres's turn to go wide-eyed.

Torin asked, "What does this new position entail, precisely?"

"A ten percent increase in salary." Grovis smiled. "And nothing else, really, as your responsibilities and duties will remain the same otherwise. But I think you deserved more than the standard every-five-years raise."

Danthres shook her head. "Figures. I'm finally starting to like you, Grovis, and you're leaving."

"All the more reason for me to leave, then. I doubt I'd be able to maintain good will with you for more than a day in any event."

"Good point."

"As for the final detective spot, that will go to Horran from Mermaid Precinct. As to who will partner with whom, I will leave that to my successor." Grovis nodded to Dru.

"Uh, yeah, okay." He blew out a breath. "Guess I need to figure some shit out."

Grovis clapped his hands once. Danthres was starting to think that was something they trained upper-class twits to do. "In any case, I must—"

Bonce, one of the guards assigned to the castle, came running in. "'Scuse me, Lieutenants, but we got us three dead bodies in the Dancing Seagull."

Torin put his head in his hands. "They couldn't wait until dark like usual?"

Suddenly, the room was silent. With amusement, Danthres realized that they were all waiting for Osric to tell someone what to do. She looked at Dru. Dru was looking at Grovis, who was also looking at Dru.

"Shit," Dru said, "this is my decision now, ain't it?"

Grovis shook his head. "Formally, no, as my duties as captain don't truly end until this shift is completed, but I'm not sure how the partnerships are to be divvied—"

"Oh, lord and lady, Torin and I will take it." Danthres got to her feet. "After a week of teleporting and testifying at the castle in Velessa, I'm more than ready to sink my teeth into a triple."

"Agreed," Torin said.

Danthres reached down to her desk and folded the parchment up and put it away in her desk. Javian's letter could wait until later, when she'd had an ale or two in her and so would be in the proper frame of mind to decipher his handwriting.

As she folded it, though, she caught one thing he wrote: "It was good to see you doing something you love. You seem happy, Thressa. I wouldn't have believed you could be happy twenty years ago."

Looking over at Torin, she smiled. *I am happy. Imagine that.*

"Let's go," Torin said. "We can collect Boneen en route."

"After you, partner."

LORD DOVAL'S SECRETARY HAD FETCHED HIM A MUG OF FRUIT JUICE WHILE HE was talking with the people from the Castle Guard. He gratefully took it as he sat down at the desk that had very briefly been his brother's.

He couldn't believe Blayk had been so *stupid*. The plan the two of them and their sister Juliana had worked out was a *long-term* plan. Yes, it would've taken years, but it would've *worked*. To go to the extreme of poisoning Father and trying to kill the king and queen and barreling into Cliff's End like a troll in a china shop was absurd and doomed to fail. They'd *told* him that, but did he listen? No, he was the oldest, he knew best.

Idiot.

If their family was to rule all of Flingaria, they were going to need to be smart about it. The days of tyrants barging in and taking over were in the past, and needed to stay dead alongside the Elf Queen and Chalmraik the Foul. It was a new era, and it called for a subtler hand.

He grabbed a few slates off the desk that Blayk had left behind, with some figures compiled by Teffeth. At least, Blayk had the right idea about *some* things. These plans for strengthening the castle and the port were good ones, and would serve them well when the time came.

Doval sipped his fruit juice and got to work.

ABOUT THE AUTHOR

Kᴇɪᴛʜ R.A. DᴇCᴀɴᴅɪᴅᴏ ɪs ᴀ ᴡʜɪᴛᴇ ᴍᴀʟᴇ ɪɴ ʜɪs ᴇᴀʀʟʏ ꜰᴏʀᴛɪᴇs, ᴀᴘᴘʀᴏxɪ-mately 200 pounds. He was last seen in the wilds of the Bronx, New York, though he is often sighted in other locales. Usually he is armed with a laptop computer, which some have classified as a deadly weapon. Through use of this laptop, he has inflicted more than fifty novels, as well as an indeterminate number of short stories, comic books, nonfiction, novellas, and anthologies on an unsuspecting reading public. Many of these are set in the milieus of television shows, movies, games, and comic books, among them Star Trek, Cars, Doctor Who, Supernatural, World of Warcraft, Orphan Black, Alien, Marvel Comics, and many more. We have received information confirming that more stories involving Torin, Danthres, and the city-state of Cliff's End can be found in the novels *Unicorn Precinct, Goblin Precinct, Gryphon Precinct,* and the forthcoming *Mermaid Precinct, Phoenix Precinct,* and *Manticore Precinct,* as well as the short-story collection *Tales from Dragon Precinct.* His other recent crimes against humanity include the urban fantasy novel *A Furnace Sealed;* the Orphan Black coffee-table book *Classified Clone Report;* the Alien novel *Isolation;* the *Tales of Asgard* trilogy of prose novels featuring Marvel's Thor, Sif, and the Warriors Three; short stories in the anthologies *Aliens: Bug Hunt,* the two *Baker Street Irregulars* volumes, *The Best of Bad-Ass Faeries, The Best of Defending the Future, Joe Ledger: Unstoppable, Nights of the Living Dead, The X-Files: Trust No One,* among others; and writing about pop culture for Tor.com and Patreon. If you see DeCandido, do not approach him, but call for back-up immediately. He is often seen in the company of a suspicious-looking woman who goes by the street name of "Wrenn," as well as several as-yet-unidentified cats. A full dossier can be found at DeCandido.net.

Bonus story:

"Chaos Theory"

In Gryphon Precinct, Lady Meerka mentioned a case involving a Hamnau Gem. As a special bonus in this new edition of the novel, we present, for the first time ever, the story of that particular case.

He holds the gem and concentrates, and then he's someone else. He stands near the shops on the far end of Jorbin's Way, no longer in his home on Covura Way.

He smiles. Now it can begin.

"I'M TELLING YOU, I DIDN'T KILL THAT WOMAN!"

Lieutenant Torin ban Wyvald looked up at his partner, Lieutenant Danthres Tresyllione. Torin was seated across from the man who'd made that declaration, a cooper who managed one of the larger barrelers in Cliff's End. Danthres was standing, leaning against the wall of the interrogation room.

"You've said that several times, Mr. Lacque," Danthres said. "And yet, several people saw you kill the woman, and the M.E.'s peel-back spell also clearly showed you walking up to her and breaking her neck."

"That's insane! I don't remember anything like that!" Lacque was gesticulating madly from the other side of the battered old table. "I don't even know *how* to break a neck!"

"And yet, here we are," Danthres said.

"Do you have anything to say in mitigation of your act?" Torin asked.

"What act? I don't know the woman! I've never killed anyone! I was in the shop this morning, and then the next thing I knew, you people were taking me here!"

"Enough of this." Danthres pushed herself off the wall and moved toward the exit. "Let's go."

With a sigh, Torin got to his feet and followed her out of the room.

"I didn't do it!" Lacque cried as Torin left.

As he entered the squadroom, Torin spied one of the guards assigned to the castle. "Abrik, could you escort the prisoner down to the hole?"

Nodding, Abrik moved toward the interrogation room to carry out his instructions. Once they were gone, Danthres and Torin were alone in the squadroom. The other four detectives were out on cases, Captain Osric was no longer in his office, and Sergeant Jonas had left early to tend to his sick wife.

As she sat at her desk, Danthres said, "I told you interrogating him was a waste of time. We already have everything we need from the witnesses and the peel-back. Lacque killed that woman."

With a heavy sigh, Torin sat at his desk, which abutted hers. "I was hoping at the very least he would tell us who the woman is. We still don't have an identification for her."

Danthres snorted. "Revealing her name would spoil his amnesia narrative."

"I suppose."

He was about to say something else, when a sound rarely heard in the castle echoed from the corridor outside the squadroom entrance: Captain Osric's laughter.

The braying laugh preceded the man himself, who entered the squadroom accompanied by Sir Palrik, one of the nobles currently serving as chief military advisor to the lord and lady, and a dwarven woman in red leather armor with hair to match. It was a very similar shade of crimson to Torin's own long hair and thick beard.

Getting to his feet, a huge grin on his face, Torin cried out, "Red!"

The dwarf, whose full name was Hemredit, looked over at him, her grin then matching his, though hers had many fewer teeth.

"Xinf's feet," she said, "is that you, Red?"

"Indeed, it is!"

"Wasn't sure with all that fuzz on your face. Whose stupid idea was it for you to grow a beard?"

"Mine." Torin shrugged. "I like the look of it."

Osric said, "He attempted being without it once five years ago. It went badly."

"I kept forgetting to shave daily, and my face rather looked like a ravaged forest."

Danthres also got to her feet and said, "I gather you two know each other, as Torin isn't in the habit of identifying people solely by hair color."

Hemredit gave Osric a sidelong glance. "I see what you mean when you say they're detectives. She figured that out almost immediately!"

Osric laughed again, which made twice in the last year or so that Torin had heard him do so. "That's why I promoted her a decade ago when I took the job. Tresyllione, this is Hemredit. She served under me during the war along with Sir Palrik and ban Wyvald. Hemredit, this is Lieutenant Danthres Tresyllione, my finest detective."

Torin shot Osric a look at that—usually he referred to the pair of them as his best detectives. Not that he objected to Danthres receiving greater praise, he was simply surprised, as that wasn't Osric's usual style.

Then again, living comrades from the elven war were rare.

"You're from Sorlin, aren't you?" Hemredit asked, regarding Danthres more directly.

"That was a long time ago," was all Danthres said in response.

"You're better off. I was down there recently. Horrible place. All that sea water." She shuddered.

"So naturally," Torin said with a grin, "you came to a port town."

"And getting away from the docks, believe me," Hemredit added quickly. "Bad enough I had to sail here."

"Hemredit," Osric said, "is working a job. She finds things for people."

Danthres asked, "You any good at it?"

Torin winced. Danthres's tone was even more snide than usual. No doubt she was bridling under Hemredit's initial comment, not to mention her disdain for the land where Danthres came from. A haven for halfbreeds like her fleeing elven purity laws, Sorlin was where Danthres had spent most of her life. Fifteen years ago, she left for reasons that Torin had never been able to pry out of his partner.

Luckily, Hemredit took the question in stride. "I haven't starved to death yet, so I must be."

"Given how often people lose things," Torin added, "I can't imagine a shortage of clients. Besides, as I recall, you were the one who found Fankell's sword that time."

"Certainly he was never going to," Hemredit said. "Fankell would've lost his head if it wasn't attached."

Palrik finally spoke up. "As pleasant as it is to reminisce with old friends, I must take my leave. There is a meeting I have been asked to attend, and Lady Meerka will be quite cross if I am late."

Hemredit gave the noble a short bow. "It was a pleasure to see you again, Major."

Waving her off, Palrik said, "Now, now, Hemredit, I'm no longer an officer. And the pleasure was mine."

With that, Sir Palrik took his leave.

Osric's face grew serious upon the noble's departure. "I take it that our murderer wasn't forthcoming with the identity of his victim? Or better still, a confession?"

Torin shook his head. "Neither, I'm afraid."

"I doubt the magistrate will waste any time condemning him even without the confession. Too many witnesses, including Boneen," she said, referring to the magickal examiner; his Inanimate Residue Spell had identified Lacque as the killer.

"Pity. It would be good to at least alert that poor woman's family." Osric scratched his chin. "Hemredit, I'm afraid we must all get back to work."

"As it happens, I have work to do here in Cliff's End of my own— I only stopped by because I couldn't resist the chance to see you and the major again. Didn't realize I'd get Red thrown in the bargain." She added that with another gap-toothed grin at Torin.

Danthres asked, "What work might that be?"

Hemredit's smile fell. "Mine. I'm sorry, Lieutenant, but my clients prefer discretion."

Holding up both hands, Danthres said, "My apologies. I merely thought we might be able to aid you."

"Very considerate, but unnecessary," she said tersely.

Danthres added, "It's the least I can offer to someone who made Osric laugh in my presence, which is about as common an occurrence as a vampire."

Torin chuckled at Danthres's comment, since vampires had been wiped out five years ago. Hemredit's face softened as well, though Osric's scowl deepened.

"I appreciate the offer, Lieutenant, truly, but I've barely begun my search." She turned to face Osric. "I'll see you at nineteen?"

"Definitely," Osric said.

"Good to see you again, Red," Hemredit said to Torin as she turned toward the door.

"You as well, Red," Torin replied as she took her leave. Then he turned to Osric. "What's at nineteen?"

"Hemredit's staying at the Dog and Duck. She invited Sir Palrik and I to join her for a drink there—you're welcome, as well, ban Wyvald." He looked past him to his partner. "You may join us as well, Tresyllione."

Chuckling, Danthres said, "I'll pass, thanks. Listening to you four carry on about the war sounds about as exciting as a dinner with Grovis's family. Enjoy yourselves, though."

Still riding the thrill of the last time, he once again activates the gem, and now he is walking down Meerka Way near Celinda Pass. He turns onto the smaller thoroughfare as soon as he sees the perfect target.

TORIN FINALLY STUMBLED INTO THE SQUADROOM ALMOST AN HOUR INTO HIS shift. He immediately went to the pantry to make himself some tea.

"Good night?" Danthres asked.

"What I recall of it, yes," Torin said in a weak voice. "Red can still throw back ale as well as she could a decade ago, it seems. She barely seemed affected by the time we closed the tavern down."

"And you made it back home by yourself?"

"Actually, no." Torin sighed as he poured water over the tea leaves. "Red allowed me to sleep in her rooms at the Dog and Duck. Why isn't the water hot?" Looking under the pot, he saw that no one had lit the twigs that were used to boil the water.

"Jonas's wife has taken a turn for the worse. And I already assumed it was a good night because Osric sent word that he's taking a sick day as well. Dru and Hawk are still trying to find their thief, and Iaian and the fish went out on a call first thing."

"Iaian and who?"

Danthres blinked. "Grovis, of course."

"Right."

"Torin, *you* were the one who first started referring to him as 'the fish' back when he joined the squad after Linder was killed. How much ale *did* you drink?"

"All of it." He tried to use the flint to light up the twigs to heat the water.

After the fifth attempt, Danthres took pity on him. "Oh, stop that, you'll rip your fingers off at this rate. I'll make your tea, go sit at your desk and try not to die."

"Thank you," Torin said with all the emotion he could muster—which wasn't all that much.

He sat at his desk, staring at the view of the Forest of Nimvale out the squadroom window, not thinking about much of anything at all until Danthres brought him his tea.

"'Scuse, Lieutenants?"

Looking up from his tea, Torin saw a guard standing in the doorway. It took him several seconds to place him as Yorn Bonce, one of the guards assigned to the castle. "Yes, Bonce?"

"There's three people here to see you two."

"To see *us*?" Danthres asked.

"You two caught the case with that woman who got killed? Arrested a guy named Mas Lacque?"

Danthres nodded.

"They said they wanted the detectives in charge of that, so yeah, they wanna see you two."

"Send them in," Torin said.

Danthres shot him a look. "What possible—"

Two young men and one young woman walked in. They all wore clothes made of simple linen, cheap and easy to obtain, but the clothes were well kept, so they were probably middle-class denizens of Dragon Precinct.

One of the men asked, "Excuse us, are you the ones who arrested Mas?"

"If you mean Mas Lacque, yes," Torin said. "I'm Lieutenant Torin ban Wyvald, and this is Lieutenant Danthres Tresyllione."

"You've made a mistake."

"I doubt that," Danthres said. "Half a dozen witnesses saw him kill that woman, and our magickal examiner performed a peel-back that proved it."

The other man said, "I don't know what a peel-back is, but it's wrong, whatever it is."

Danthres gave the man a look that made him cringe. It was a look Danthres usually gave to suspects, and it sometimes cowed them into confessing. In this case, the youngster simply took a step back.

Torin spoke up before Danthres said something untoward to an innocent citizen of Cliff's End. "The peel-back is more formally known as an Inanimate Residue Spell. It shows what happened in a particular location some time in the recent past. I'm afraid it's never been wrong." That wasn't entirely true—there were plenty of times where the peel-back was inconclusive for some reason. However, it never provided false information, only sometimes incomplete information. Torin didn't think it politic to get into that much depth on the subject with civilians.

"Look," the woman said, "I know wizards are supposed to know everything and not lie, but I don't believe it. Mas *couldn't* have killed *anyone*. He's not capable."

"It's been my experience," Danthres said quietly, "that anyone is capable of murder given the right set of circumstances."

"These weren't those, trust me," the first man said. "We were in the Ogre's Breath a year ago, and a brawl broke out."

Torin snorted. A brawl broke out in the OB on a nightly basis.

"Mas couldn't even hit anyone. He was completely helpless. They say he strangled that woman, and he wouldn't even know *how* to strangle someone. He couldn't even slap someone properly, much less throw a punch."

"We appreciate the testimonial," Torin said, "and if you leave us your addresses, we will make sure the magistrate gets the information so that you may speak at his trial."

That earned Torin another look from Danthres, but the three people provided that information and then took their leave.

"We know he did it, Torin," Danthres said. "Just because his friends are buying into his shit story doesn't mean it's any more true."

"Perhaps, but at least—"

He was interrupted by one of the youth squad walking in the door. It was a tall young girl, an orphan who lived on the streets of Goblin Precinct, and who ran errands for the Castle Guard by way of staying out of trouble.

"Where's everyone?" she asked.

"We're right here," Torin said, gathering up a smile.

"What is it?" Danthres asked.

"'S'a body down by Celinda Pass."

"I suppose we shall have to take that?" Torin asked.

"Well, we could leave it be—it's not as if Osric or Jonas is here to say otherwise—but that would hardly be fair to the victim, would it?"

Torin knew that Danthres was humoring him—and in truth, he would never leave a body unattended. As Danthres had so eloquently said when they first partnered up a decade ago, deaths were the most important investigations for the lieutenants of the Castle Guard to perform. The detectives spoke for those who could no longer speak for themselves.

After getting Bonce to mind the squadroom until one of the other detectives returned, the pair of them ambled down Meerka Way through the mansions of Unicorn Precinct and into the more-jammed-together structures of Dragon Precinct.

"What've we got?" Danthres asked as she approached the cul-de-sac of Celinda Pass.

Several guards with a dragon crest on their black leather armor were holding a crowd of gawkers back. One of them, Jared, stepped forward at Danthres and Torin's approach. "'Ey, Lieutenants. We got a nasty one." He pointed at the young woman lying dead on the ground. "Woman's name is Lokyra. She was just walkin' down the street to the hat store down the pass, an' some other lady walked up to her and broke her neck."

That got Torin's attention. "Did she say anything?"

Jared shook his head. "Nah, jus' walked up, killed 'er, an' walked off."

"That seems—eerily familiar."

Danthres was kneeling over the body. "That's not the only thing. Look at this."

Torin walked over to look more closely at the dead body. Besides her head being at an impossible angle, Torin noticed that she was human, young, female, and with curly blonde hair.

"She looks very much like the last victim."

"Yes." Danthres rose to her feet. "And that killer is still in the hole."

Turning to Jared, Torin asked, "Did you send for the M.E.?"

Jared nodded. "Same girl I sent t'get you, I sent t'get him."

"Good." Then he caught sight of a familiar set of tresses in the crowd. "Red?"

Danthres shot Torin a look, then followed his gaze into the crowd. "Is that your dwarf friend?" Said friend was waving at him.

Nodding, Torin spoke to the guard closest to her, "Let her through, please."

The guard pushed a few people aside, and Hemredit walked over. "You look like shit, Red."

"Oh good," Torin said wryly, "I'd hate to feel this bad and have it be a secret. I should have stopped after the tenth ale."

Danthres's eyes went wide. "Ten?"

"More like a score," Hemredit said with a chuckle.

Trying to yank the conversation back to the case, Torin asked, "Did you perchance see anything, Red?"

"Afraid not, I just happened to be in the area, following up a lead on my own job."

The next time, he activates the gem and finds himself on Ruber's Way inside someone's house. He's wearing a cloak and armor now, which he thinks is just perfect. A woman calls out a name as he leaves the house, but he ignores it while he searches for another.

BONEEN'S PEEL-BACK WAS ALSO A REPEAT: LOKYRA WAS APPROACHED BY A woman she didn't seem to recognize who stood in front of her, reached out, snapped her neck, and walked off — the same as Lacque and that other poor woman.

By the end of the shift, Jared arrived at the castle with a woman named Gima in custody, who matched the description Boneen and the witnesses had provided of the murderer.

"What am I doing here?" Gima asked from the very same seat that Lacque had been in.

"This morning," Danthres said, "you were on Celinda Pass—"

"No, I wasn't. I mean, I was near Celinda Pass, but I never—"

"Yes, you were." Danthres stood on the other side of the table and bent over, hands on the battered wood. "Several witnesses saw you, and a wizard did a spell that proved conclusively that you were there just long enough to kill a woman named Lokyra."

"What!? That's not—I mean—I've never *hurt* anyone before! I don't even know *how* to kill someone! I mean, I guess if I had a sword, maybe, but—"

"Lokyra's neck was snapped," Torin said.

"Do I look like I could snap someone's neck? How do you even *do* that?"

Danthres frowned. "Do what?"

"Snap someone's neck? I mean, I don't—*this is insane!*"

The interview continued on in that vein until the detectives eventually gave up and went back into the squadroom, sitting at their desks across from each other.

"We have the evidence, we should put her in the hole." Even as she said the words, Danthres sounded less than convinced to Torin.

For his part, Torin was completely unconvinced. "Danthres, I believe Gima when she says she's never snapped someone's neck. She was genuinely horrified by the very notion."

Danthres let out a very long sigh. "Yes. Yes, she was. And it's also more than a little bizarre that two people have come at us with the same story that flies in the face of the evidence."

"Lieutenant Tresyllione?"

Both Danthres and Torin turned toward the voice, which belonged to another of the youth squad. "Sergeant Jonas says for you to come quick."

Torin frowned. "I thought Jonas was staying home with his wife today."

"So did I." Danthres turned to the youth. "Where are we supposed to come quick to?"

"Ruber's Way."

Getting up from his chair, Torin said, "Jonas lives on Ruber's Way, so perhaps it's something with his wife."

When the pair arrived at that thoroughfare, Jonas was standing with several guards from Dragon Precinct, who were holding back a crowd of people who did *not* look happy.

The sergeant looked stricken. "Torin, Danthres, I don't know what's happening, but all these people are saying that I killed that woman!"

Jonas was pointing at the center of the road, where Torin saw another dead woman with blonde hair.

Jared brought a dwarf out from the crowd, and once they got through, Torin realized it was Hemredit. "Red? What are you doing here?"

Hemredit, looked abashed. "I saw the whole thing, I'm afraid. Your green-cloaked friend there just walked up and killed that woman. I'm sorry, Red, but he did!"

That got the crowd going.

"Damn right, he did!"

"'E killed Terise!"

"Lousy guards! Get rid of 'em all!"

"Arrest 'im!"

"Bet they won't!"

"Stinkin' Cloaks!"

The guards from Dragon tried to calm the crowd, but they were emboldened by Hemredit's direct statement.

Jonas looked even more devastated. "I don't remember anything. I was caring for Mandy, and then the next thing I knew I was here. I don't even know who that woman is."

"Terise, apparently," Torin said. "We need to get Boneen here to confirm with a peel-back."

Someone threw a battered old metal mug that just missed Jonas's ear.

"Somehow," Danthres said, "I don't think we'll be able to clear this alley any time soon."

Holding up both hands over his head, Torin tried to bellow over the complaining of the crowd. "Good people, please! We need to investigate this crime and—"

"Don't need to investigate nothin'! We saw it! That Cloak killed Terise!"

"Perhaps, but we need to have our magickal examiner come in and—"

"Wizards won't do nothin'!"

"Justice for Terise!"

"People, please, we—" were the last words Torin said before something flew out of the crowd and hit him on the head.

WHEN HE WOKE UP, HE WAS SITTING ON THE GROUND, LEANING UP AGAINST a building. A healer was standing over him.

"What—what happened?" he asked.

"You'll be fine, you will," the healer said. "Got other folks to attend to, I do. 'Scuse."

The healer moved off and then Danthres stood over him. Her left eye was swollen shut. "You look like shit."

"You're not looking particularly good yourself."

She waved it off. "One of the rioters got a lucky punch in. He's in the hole now, as is the one who threw the rock at your head, and a few others. The rest got dispersed. Sergeant Grint sent most of Dragon out here to take care of it. Careful!"

That last was added as Torin tried to get to his feet. Danthres offered him a gloved hand, which he gladly took.

"Ooof!" they both cried as she hauled him to his feet.

"Bad enough I'm still recovering from our debauchery last night, but now my head is—" Then his eyes went wide. "Red! Where is she?"

"No idea. She disappeared during the riot. Can't say as I entirely blame her, it got pretty ugly. But I want to know why she was at *two* of the crime scenes."

"As do I."

THE SHIFT WAS ALMOST OVER BY THE TIME BONEEN FINALLY ARRIVED TO perform the peel-back.

Unfortunately, that only confirmed that Jonas appeared to have done the deed.

"It is exactly as it was for the other two," the M.E. said. "The sergeant simply walked up to the victim, grabbed her by the throat and snapped it, then dropped her corpse to the ground and walked away."

Osric had shown up while Boneen was performing the spell and heard his report. "This is bad."

"Captain," Jonas started, but Osric cut him off.

"I know, Jonas. You couldn't have done this. But the evidence is rather overwhelming."

"As it was for our last two suspects," Torin said. "Yet these are ordinary citizens, not ones who are prone to violence."

"Oh come on, Torin," Danthres said. "You know as well as I that anyone can be provoked to violence given the right set of circumstances."

"Yes, and when you told Lacque's friends that, I agreed with you. But that was when we only had one such murder. Now we've had three in three days, of the *same type*, against strangers."

Danthres sighed. "True. Usually when someone not prone to violence becomes so, it's due to someone they know or care about. This manner of killing—" She shuddered. "I don't like it. And I don't like that your war buddy has been present for two of these killings."

"Hemredit was here?" Osric asked.

Torin nodded. "And at the Celinda Pass murder."

"She knows something," Danthres said. "She might even be involved."

"I doubt that," Osric said.

"With respect, Captain, you're seeing her through the blinders of war nostalgia. So are you, Torin. For all we know, she was near the first scene as well."

"Actually, no, she wasn't." Torin recalled the conversation in the early part of the evening at the Dog and Duck. "She was still on the Garamin Sea when that first woman was killed. Her boat didn't arrive at the docks until that evening."

"Fine, but I still think we should talk to her," Danthres said.

Torin nodded. "Agreed."

The timechimes rang seventeen, signaling the end of the shift. Osric said, "All right. Jonas, I'm sorry, but I'm going to have to take you back to the castle and place you under arrest."

"Captain, please," Jonas said, with tears welling in his eyes, "I didn't do this."

"I know that, Sergeant," Osric said formally, "but given what just happened here, if I let you go—"

"It's not just that," Jonas said, "it's Mandy. She's still ill, and I need to be home caring for her."

Osric rubbed his cheek, then said, "All right, you can go home, but you're going to have a guard with you at all times." He snapped his fingers and summoned Jared over. "Take Sergeant Jonas with you back to Dragon, tell him I want a guard to escort him home and stay the night. I'm going to have a healer sent to care for his wife, also, but aside from that healer, no one is to be let into the house who isn't with the Castle Guard."

"Will do, Captain."

As Jared led the miserable sergeant away, Danthres regarded Osric with skepticism. "Who's going to pay for a healer to sit with Mandy all night long?"

"The budget will cover it. And if any of those copper hoarders in the other wing of the castle wish to complain, they may do so at their leisure."

Danthres grinned. "If they do, can I watch?"

Osric chuckled. "I'll track Hemredit down, and we'll meet with her first thing in the morning. You two go home and get some rest."

Those last three words were music to Torin's ears. "Absolutely," he said, putting his hand to his throbbing head.

This next time he finds himself in a man wearing smooth silk instead of cheap linen. He smiles. Royalty, perhaps, or at least someone who puts "Sir" before his name. The noble was already walking down Meerka Way, and he contin- ues, waiting for the right person to present herself.

As usual, Torin was late arriving for his shift the following day. He was surprised to see Boneen in the squadroom, a place he preferred not to haunt.

"What brings you here, Boneen?"

"A meeting, one I wasn't eager to take in the first place."

"I'm sorry?"

Osric came out of his office with Danthres. "I left a note with Olaf at the Dog and Duck for Hemredit to meet me here today. She left a message with one of the guards here that she was meeting with Boneen this morning, and she would come by afterward. I brought Boneen up here, because her meeting with us is of more import."

"In all honesty," Boneen said, "I'd be happy to avoid it all together. But I did promise to meet with her, for reasons passing understanding, so I will remain."

Torin smiled. Boneen may have been a cranky old wizard, but he was also a mage of his word.

Hemredit was escorted in a few minutes later by a guard. "Hello again, everyone. I was told Boneen was here?"

Waddling forward toward the dwarf, the M.E. said, "I am Boneen. You must be Hemredit."

"Thank you for agreeing to meet with me. Is there somewhere private we may talk?"

"I'm afraid," Osric said, "that will have to wait. I told Boneen to wait for you here because our business with you takes precedence."

Hemredit winced. "I'm sorry, General, but my duties to my employer are—"

"Of absolutely no interest to me."

Torin stepped toward the dwarf. "Red, I'm afraid we have questions for you that must be asked."

"And I'm happy to answer them, Red, but after I speak to Boneen. It's urgent."

"So is our business," Torin said.

Danthres then spoke up. "You were at two crime scenes over the past two days. What's more, you were at two *remarkably similar* crime scenes. You see, we've had three murders over the past three days, all of young blonde-haired women, all by people who didn't know them, all by people who do not have any kind of violent history."

"One of them," Osric put in, "is a sergeant in the Castle Guard whose reputation is beyond reproach."

"Why were you at those scenes, Red?" Torin asked.

Hemredit stared at each of them in turn, and then took a breath. "I'm sorry, Red, I can't discuss it. My employer hired me for my discretion. I can't very well babble about it to all of you."

"Actually, you can," Danthres said, "and you will, or there will be consequences."

"I'm simply doing my job!"

"So is an assassin, yet when one kills a person, we still imprison her."

"I haven't killed anyone!" Hemredit shook her head, her red tresses bouncing back and forth. "Dammit, you don't understand."

"Actually," Osric said, "it's you who do not understand. You called me 'General' a minute ago, but I'm no longer a military commander. Now I'm properly addressed as 'Captain,' for I lead the Castle Guard. Our mandate is to maintain law and order within the demesne. That mandate gives us very broad powers when it comes to investigating violations of the lord and lady's law."

Hemredit frowned. "What does that mean, exactly, Gen— Sorry, *Captain*?"

Torin put a hand on her shoulder. "It means, Red, that if you do not answer our questions, we are within our rights to imprison you for impeding our investigation into these three murders."

Blowing out a long breath, Hemredit said, "Fine, I'll tell you. I was hired by a—a business owner in Barlin who wished me to retrieve an item he'd lost."

"And what item was that?" Danthres asked.

"One of his Hamnau Gems."

"What!?" That was Boneen, who hadn't been particularly engaged in the conversation, but sat up and took notice at the mention of this gem. "That's not possible. All six Hamnau Gems were destroyed."

"What is a Hamnau Gem?" Danthres asked.

"Nelg Hamnau was an apprentice of Chalmraik the Foul," Boneen said. "He created a spell that would enable a person to take possession of another person's body. Hamnau was killed, and the spell was lost, except in the gems he embedded with the spell. But after Chalmraik's death, the Brotherhood of Wizards outlawed the spell and had all half-dozen gems destroyed."

Wincing, Hemredit said, "You're correct in that six of the gems were destroyed, but Hamnau actually made ten of them. You see, my client is Hamnau's nephew. He has two of the remaining four—he thinks the other two are in Velessa."

"He *thinks*?" Boneen put a hand to his head. "This is unbelievable. Those gems are incredibly dangerous. With one of those someone could—"

Danthres interrupted, "Take possession of someone's body and commit murder, thus framing the other person?"

Boneen sighed. "Yes."

Danthres moved toward Hemredit. "You waited until *now* to tell us this?"

"I'm sorry, Lieutenant, but I was given strict instructions—"

"I don't give two shits about your instructions! Two people have *died* since you arrived in Cliff's End—both those deaths could have been avoided if you'd told us what you were doing!"

"I had no idea that the gems were the cause—"

"I think you had a pretty good idea after Lokyra's death, and certainly after Terise yesterday."

Osric stepped between his current subordinate and his former one. "That's enough, both of you. Hemredit, you will tell us everything you know about this gem, right now. Failure to do so will result in your immediate imprisonment, am I clear?"

"Absolutely, General. Sorry…*Captain*." Hemredit reached into a pouch on her belt and pulled out a charm. "My client gave me this to track the gem. It kept alerting me, but then nothing else after the initial alert."

Boneen held out a hand. "May I see that, please?"

"Of course." Hemredit handed the charm over.

Turning it over in his hands, Boneen said, "As I suspected. This is not a tracking charm, it's an alert. It goes off once in the presence of a magickal item of sufficiently great power. Not just a Hamnau Gem, but any powerful item, like a Keefda Stone or a Casdday Gem, would also set it off."

"Oh." Hemredit packed a certain amount of annoyance into that one word, Torin noticed.

Handing it back to the dwarf, Boneen went on: "However, it's also likely the only method available to your client—whose name I will not allow you to leave this castle without providing, by the way."

Swallowing, Hemredit said, "If I must."

"You must. Possession of a Hamnau Gem is considered a crime by the brotherhood, and I assure you, the punishments they can enact are far worse than simple imprisonment or execution." Boneen waddled over to Iaian's chair—he and Grovis were out on a case—and sat in it with a huff. "In any event, there is no way to properly track a Hamnau Gem. It's one of a multitude of reasons why they're banned."

Torin sighed. "Then we must figure out another way to find the perpetrator. Red, was there anyone you noticed who was at both crime scenes?"

Hemredit shook her head. "Not that I saw, but I'm afraid I was more focused on searching for the gem. Besides, most people are too damn tall for me to see faces."

At that, Torin chuckled.

Meanwhile, Danthres was walking over to the picture window and summoning Ep, the imp who kept all the Castle Guard's files. The glass of the window twisted and reformed into the imp's ugly face.

"I need a map of Cliff's End, please, Ep."

"Of course," Ep's reedy voice said, and a map sprung out of the creature's mouth.

Danthres unrolled it, stared at it, rolled it back up, and shoved it back in the imp's mouth. "I said Cliff's End, Ep, not Iaron."

"Oh, sorry." Ep spit out another map.

Unrolling this one, she said, "*Thank* you."

As the imp's face disappeared, Danthres took the map to her desk and spread it out across the wood.

"What are you thinking, Tresyllione?" Osric asked.

"All the witnesses pointed to the killer, so we didn't ask further questions, and we'll never find those people again to ask follow-ups. So we look for other ways into this. Our killer has already proven to have a preference for killing young human blondes. Perhaps that's not the only pattern to the murders."

Torin walked around to her desk. "You're thinking there's a geographic pattern?"

"All the killings have been in Dragon Precinct, which is a start." She pointed at one spot on the map. "Here's where that first woman's body was found." Then she pointed at another. "There's Celinda Pass, and there's Ruber's Way," she said pointing at the third location.

Bonce came in the door, just then. "There's a body on Meerka Way! Another blonde girl!"

"Where?" Danthres asked.

"Right at the intersection of Grobb's Pass."

Danthres looked down and put a finger on that part of the map.

Torin grabbed a quill pen and drew lines connecting the four scenes. They made a perfect circle.

Osric frowned. "Get down to Meerka and Grobb's. Boneen, go with them. Let's verify that this is our Hamnau Gem killer again."

"Right," Danthres said.

BONEEN'S PEEL-BACK REVEALED THAT THE KILLER WAS SIR PALRIK.

The victim was a woman named Eriana, who was the daughter of the owners of Narra's Magick Shop.

By the time Torin, Danthres, and Boneen were finished at the crime scene—and had somewhat calmed Eriana's parents down—and returned to the castle, Sir Palrik was waiting for them.

"I'm afraid I don't understand what happened," he said without preamble as Torin and Danthres entered the squadroom.

"Why don't we go into the interrogation room?" Torin suggested, leading his former military superior into one of the aforesaid rooms.

Palrik was shaking his head. "This is just bizarre. They're telling me I killed Eriana."

"You know her?" Danthres asked. In fact, they already knew that from Eriana's parents, but it was good to get confirmation from the other end, as it were.

Nodding, Palrik said, "I frequent Narra's quite regularly. She was always very kind to me. I don't recall seeing her today, though. I was walking to the castle from Abelard's—I'd had breakfast there. I—" He tilted his head. "I don't recall actually walking here, though. I left the eatery, and then I was here—and I can't remember what happened between."

Torin said, "As far as we can determine, you were possessed by a killer who has a magick gem."

"Oh dear. That's—that's *terrible*. That poor girl. And they say I did it?"

"With this gem, yes."

Palrik looked down. Torin saw tears welling in his eyes. "Oh dear, oh dear."

They spoke for a bit longer, then left him, returning to the squadroom.

Osric entered from the main door. "I've just been speaking with Lord Albin. He's very upset about Sir Palrik, and apparently so are the Brotherhood of Wizards, about both Eriana's death and that a Hamnau Gem is involved. Lord Ythran went on at quite some length to Lord Albin on the subject, and he went on at me." The captain's tone made it abundantly clear how little he enjoyed that particular conversation with the lord of the demesne.

"We've got two innocent people in the hole, another under house arrest, and a fourth in the interrogation room," Danthres said. "This has to stop. Now."

Torin said, "We need to find the gem."

Hemredit had been sitting at Iaian's desk, and she finally spoke up. "We should search with my charm within that circle Lieutenant Tresyllione found."

"Agreed," Danthres said, "but we should do more than that. We need bait."

Torin frowned. "Bait?"

"We need a glamour and a charm." Danthres turned to Osric. "How serious is Lord Albin about wanting this person?"

Unhesitatingly, the captain said, "Serious enough to approve the purchase of a glamour and a charm. What did you have in mind?"

He sees the tenseness around him as he takes over another person, standing on Oveer Pass. The people are all irritable and cranky, bumping into each other.

He loves it.

A few minutes later — after someone yells at him for walking too close — he spies another blonde woman. She, like the others, must die.

As he walks up to her, she grabs his wrist with one hand, and holds up a charm with the other.

"Got you."

TORIN RAN TOWARD WHERE DANTHRES HAD GRABBED A MAN BY THE WRIST and activated the Mabry Charm, which would freeze all magick in place when activated. It was also incredibly expensive, and Torin suspected that renting one would have never been approved had Sir Palrik not been one of those victimized by this murder spree.

The man whose wrist she'd grabbed looked frightened.

"What have you done?" he cried out as he struggled, but Danthres — who, thanks to the glamour, looked like a blonde human woman wearing a silk kimono — would not relinquish her grip.

Then she deactivated the glamour, and appeared as her usual half-elven, armored, cloaked self, complete with swollen-shut left eye. The man stopped struggling.

The crowd seemed displeased. "Filthy Cloaks, harassin' innocent folks!"

"Justice for Terise!"

"Justice for Lokyra!"

"Get outta here, you filthy Cloaks!"

Torin regarded Danthres with concern. "We should take our leave, and soon."

Nodding, Danthres glowered at the would-be murderer. "You will take us to your natural form, right now."

"What are you talking about? I'm just a normal person who was walking down—"

Danthres interrupted. "What's your name?"

"I'm sorry?"

"It's not a difficult question. What is your name?"

The man hesitated, which was enough for her.

"C'mon, Torin, let's find Hemredit and see if she can locate the gem without him."

Just then the woman herself came running up, squeezing between two annoyed onlookers. "Red! There you are! Ah, and Lieutenant Tresyllione—is this him?"

"It would seem so."

"Follow me."

Torin grabbed the man's other arm, and he and his partner led the man down the thoroughfare, amidst jeers from the populace.

Hemredit led them down Covura Way, which had a few residences and almost no pedestrians. However pissed the citizenry was, they weren't angry enough to pursue them down this narrow byway.

The dwarf stood in front of one of the older houses. "The charm went off when I walked past this house."

Even as she did so, Torin felt their suspect tense. "I believe you may be correct. Red, would you be so kind as to break down the door?"

Frowning, Hemredit said, "But I'm not a member of your Castle Guard. Wouldn't that be considered a crime if I do so?"

Danthres snarled, as the suspect had gotten over his shock and was struggling again. "Only if we arrest you. Just *do* it!"

With a shrug, Hemredit walked up to the door and gave it a good kick.

The door splintered into several dozen pieces.

Torin and Danthres led their squirming suspect inside, where they found just a simple room with basic furnishings: a couch, a chair, and a small table. A clear gem sat on the latter, illuminating the room with a pale yellow glow.

A withered old man was sitting asleep on the couch.

Danthres held up the charm and closed her eyes. The person in Torin and her arms went limp, the old man woke up, and the glow faded from the gem.

"What the hell!? What happened? What am I doing here?"

"My apologies, sir," Torin said as he released the now-very-confused man who'd been possessed. "You were the victim of a possession. You're free to go, if you wish."

"I—I don't—I—"

Meanwhile, Danthres walked over to the old man and said, "I will ask you again now that you're back in your own body, what is your name?"

The man said nothing but lunged for the Hamnau Gem.

However, Hemredit was faster, and moved between him and the gem. "I'm afraid not. Its rightful owner wants it back."

Finally, the old man spoke, his voice papery thin. "Then you should hand it to me, dwarf, for I am Nelg Hamnau!"

Torin and Danthres exchanged surprised looks. "You're supposed to be dead," Danthres said.

"My final trick of magick. Obviously, it worked." He sighed. "I suppose you're going to arrest me and have me killed?"

Danthres sneered. "I'm afraid you won't get off *quite* that easy."

Hamnau stared at Torin. "What does she mean by that?"

"She means that the Brotherhood of Wizards has taken an interest in this case, given that they thought all your gems were destroyed."

"I can assure you," Danthres added, "that they will not be happy about it—nor merciful."

"Well, that's just perfect. The whole point of this was to create public chaos! There was supposed to be rioting in the streets and eventually I would reveal myself! When you caught me, I was hoping for a trial, at least, but if the Brotherhood are going to stick their noses into it…"

"Public chaos?" Torin asked, confused.

"Do you know who I was?" Hamnau asked with his croaking voice. "Do you? Hmm?"

Hemredit answered. "You were Chalmraik the Foul's minion."

"I was his *apprentice*! His *heir*! And then he *abandoned* me! Told me I wasn't worthy, can you believe that? Then he stripped me of my magickal abilities, and added them to his own. You see, the truth was, I was completely worthy, but Chalmraik, he didn't want an heir, oh no, not him. He just wanted someone whose power he could *steal*! Bastard…"

The man Hamnau had possessed said, "I'm sorry, this is too much. I'm leaving." He practically ran out the door.

Torin frowned. "So your solution to Chalmraik's betrayal was to commit murder?"

"The one piece of magick I had left was my gems. I knew that idiot nephew of mine had two of the four the Brotherhood didn't destroy, so I stole it from him and came to Cliff's End. Don't you understand?"

"I'm afraid I don't," Torin said.

"Nor do I, but I don't much care, either," Danthres said.

"Everyone talks about Chalmraik the Foul! The nastiest wizard in history, they say! Evil incarnate, they say! Scourge of Flingaria, they say! Do they ever mention me? Never! I worked my ass off for that ungrateful mage, and all he did was steal my magick and leave me to die! Well, I was going to show them. After this, everyone will know who Hamnau is—the multiple killer of blonde women who didn't get caught!"

"Ah, but you did get caught," Danthres said.

Hamnau sighed. "Indeed. Dammit. I should've been able to kill several more and frame them."

"Why blonde women?" Hemredit asked.

"What?" Hamnau looked at her, confused.

The dwarf repeated the question. "Why blonde women?"

He shrugged. "I needed all the victims to be similar, otherwise it would have just been random murders. And I don't like blonde hair."

She grabbed the old man's arms and led him toward the exit. "Normally, I'm annoyed when the brotherhood takes over a case, but in this instance, I'm perfectly happy to leave you to their tender mercies. As I said, they won't let you off as easy as the magistrate will. *He'd* just hang you."

Torin and Hemredit watched Danthres take him out. The dwarven woman then reached for the Hamnau Gem. But Torin cut her off and took the gem himself. "I'm afraid you won't be able to take this, Red."

"Why not?"

"For starters, it's evidence in our multiple-murder case. Beyond that, I suspect the brotherhood will confiscate it in the end."

"But then I won't get paid!"

Torin gave her a dubious look. "I can't believe you were foolish enough not to get paid up front."

Hemredit smiled. "Only half. The other half was to come on delivery of the gem."

"I sincerely doubt that the brotherhood will allow you to fulfill that part of your contract with the old man's nephew."

Her smile widened. "Come on, now, Red, we're old comrades. Surely—"

"It is *because* you're my old comrade that I won't let you take the gem. I would never let my old comrade get on the wrong side of the Brotherhood of Wizards."

She sighed. "That is a fair point. Ah, well, it was worth a try. I suppose returning to Barlin is out of the question."

"Nonsense, you may return to Barlin any time. Hamnau's nephew lives in Treemark."

"How did you know that?"

"You came to Cliff's End by sea. Barlin is a land journey, and the boat you came in on regularly brings goods from Treemark."

Hemredit shook her head. "You're good, Red. I see why Osric hired you."

"Come, Red, let us return to the castle and process Hamnau. Then you and I shall drink a toast to catching our killer."

"And me out ten gold." She sighed. "Ah, well, I'm sure someone in this city-state needs something found."

Torin said nothing as he led her out of the old man's house. If Hemredit made twenty gold for one job, Torin was wondering if he was in the wrong line of work…

www.ingramcontent.com/pod-product-compliance
Lightning Source LLC
Chambersburg PA
CBHW050531190726

48284CB00003B/1020